PLAYIN' WITH KNIVES . . .

"One more time, you little Meskin bastard. Where did he go?"

Paco's eyes flickered toward Slocum's shadow as he was creeping up behind the outlaw who was holding a knife to the boy's throat. "I swear I see no one, Señor!"

A fleeting second before Slocum was behind him, the robber glanced over his shoulder. He found himself staring Slocum in the face.

Slocum's left hand shot out to seize the wrist holding the bowie to Paco's neck, and when his fingers closed in an iron grip so the boy wouldn't be hurt, Slocum touched the tip of his own bowie to the cowboy's right side.

"So," Slocum hissed, "you like steel blades?"

As the words left his mouth he drove ten inches of razor-sharp iron into the outlaw . . .

"You like pickin' on kids?" Slocum snarled, his rage beyond control for an instant. "How does it feel to have your goddamn yellow guts cut out, asshole? You like sharp things?"

JAKE LOGAN

SLOCUM AND THE YELLOW ROSE OF TEXAS

JOVE BOOKS, NEW YORK

SLOCUM AND THE YELLOW ROSE OF TEXAS

A Jove Book / published by arrangement with
the author

PRINTING HISTORY
Jove edition / July 1999

The Penguin Putnam Inc. World Wide Web site address is
http://www.penguinputnam.com

ISBN: 0-515-12532-6

A JOVE BOOK®
Jove Books are published by The Berkley Publishing Group,
a division of Penguin Putnam Inc.,
375 Hudson Street, New York, New York 10014.
JOVE and the "J" design
are trademarks belonging to Penguin Putnam Inc.

PRINTED IN THE UNITED STATES OF AMERICA

10 9 8 7 6 5 4 3 2 1

1

John Slocum knew women as well as he knew horseflesh, and when he saw this golden-haired beauty for the first time, he let his gaze wander over her the way he might if he'd been considering the purchase of a top thoroughbred stallion. The woman had fine bones, skin like milk, an oval face with pouty lips, and a pair of deep blue eyes that would melt snow off the highest peak in the Rockies in the dead of winter. She came into the Velvet Slipper the way a gentle summer breeze caresses tall prairie grass, creating waves when heads turned all over the saloon to notice her arrival.

"That's Rose Miller," Sheriff Ike Dawson said, abruptly ending their conversation regarding recent train robberies in Devil's River Canyon. "Men in this part of Texas call her the Queen of the Velvet Slipper."

"She's a beauty," Slocum said, tasting his second glass of brandy, then puffing on his rum-soaked cheroot, sending a cloud of sweet smoke toward the ceiling.

"Can't prove it," the sheriff said, "but I hear rumors she's the connection between Frank Clanton and the railroad. Rose is known to keep company with Willard Clifton. He's local manager of the Texas an' Pacific Railroad office here in San Antone. I also hear she's a friend of Clanton's. Just puttin' two an' two together, only she don't never al-

1

low Clanton to come upstairs to her room. She hires a buggy an' drives off someplace to see him, an' that's when I figure she tells him about them army payrolls comin' on certain trains. Clanton ain't never robbed a train that wasn't carryin' a goodly amount of gov'ment money. Somehow he knows which trains to rob an' which ones to let pass through that Devil's River Canyon area.''

''Why hasn't the army, or the Texas Rangers, set a trap for him near this canyon?'' Slocum asked, still admiring Rose Miller's curves as she walked, hips swaying gently, toward the bar. Every eye in the room was on her, including Slocum's, and from the way Rose carried herself, she was very much aware of the attention she was getting.

''Clanton don't hit them trains in the same place. You'd have to see that rough country to understand. There's better'n fifty miles of canyon them trains have to run through to get to El Paso. There ain't enough lawmen or soldiers in the south of Texas to cover every inch of it.''

Slocum had come to San Antonio at the request of an old friend, Malcom Warren, vice president of the Texas and Pacific Railroad Company. Slocum had done some detective work for the railroads before, although it had been a few years back. When Malcom had wired him from Fort Worth, Slocum had boarded the next train south to Texas, ending up in San Antonio, where it was believed a notorious outlaw named Frank Clanton and a gang of almost a dozen desperados somehow learned about army payrolls headed for army posts farther west. Four trains had been robbed over a period of seven months, netting the robbers over forty thousand dollars. Even with half a dozen heavily armed railroad detectives riding in the baggage cars to guard the money, Clanton had been successful in every attempt. Clanton was said to be a remorseless killer, and his men were handpicked for their skill with guns and dynamite and just about any other method used to halt a locomotive. On two occasions the trains had been derailed, injuring dozens of passengers and a squad of ten soldiers riding in one baggage car when it overturned. The army was blaming the Texas and Pacific for being unable to guard valuable shipments, and the railroad put the blame on the army for being unwilling to devote enough men to ensuring the money's safe arrival.

"Odd," Slocum said, "that they'd pick the same canyon for all the robberies. Looks to me like they're pointing fingers at themselves."

Dawson nodded. "Second time it happened, I led a big posse out to comb the canyon. We found a few tracks, only they was smart enough to scatter. We followed most of 'em to the Mexican border. That's what Clanton's doin', in my opinion. He hits a train, then him an' his men break up and head for the Rio Grande, where they're safe from the law. But what don't figure is how they know when the next payroll is comin' by train. Then, just the other day, I heard Clanton knows Rose Miller. An' damn near everybody in San Antone knows Willard Clifton frequents Rose's upstairs room from time to time."

"She's a whore," Slocum said, not a question.

"More or less," Dawson replied. "She won't take no cowboys who work for day wages up to her room. She's real picky, so I hear tell. She owns part of the Velvet Slipper, so she can do whatever she chooses."

"Who's her partner? Or is there more than one?"

"A banker by the name of Herring. Sheldon Herring. He don't want too many folks to know he's a part owner in a saloon, but it's on record at the courthouse. This building belongs to him."

Slocum saw a possible connection. "What bank does Herring work for?"

"The Planters Bank. How come you to ask?"

"Do any of the payroll shipments ever get deposited at the Planters Bank before the trains pull out of San Antone?"

The sheriff shrugged. "Can't say, but I can find out soon enough. I'll ask Willard Clifton. Clifton acts real concerned about all these robberies . . . says he's afraid he'll lose his job if it happens again. But I still think he's the one tellin' Rose when the money leaves town, only maybe he does it innocent. She may be trickin' him into tellin' her what Clanton needs to know. But like I said, I can't prove none of this. It's just a bunch of rumors an' suspicion on my part.''

Slocum finally took his eyes off the lovely Rose Miller to look at Sheriff Dawson. ''I need to see this canyon where the robberies take place. Can you draw me a map?''

''I can do better than that,'' Dawson replied. ''I can take you out there, or I'll send my deputy with you. It's due west of here, maybe three days ride. The Devil's River lies betwixt the Nueces River an' the Pecos. Empty country. Flat as a tortilla, till you get to Devil's River Canyon. That's what makes it so hard to track Clanton.''

''How's that?'' Slocum asked, downing the rest of his brandy, signaling the barman for another.

''It's rocky land. That Devil's River cuts through some of the hardest blue flint rock an' limestone on earth. Hard as hell to read a horse's tracks.''

''I need to see it,'' Slocum replied. ''I may spend a few days seein' if I can find any trace of where these train robbers make their moves. Send your deputy along to guide me, only I may send him back so I can give the place a closer look.''

''Suits me,'' Dawson said.

''Before I leave, I'd like to talk to this banker by the name of Herring, and Malcom Warren asked me to pay a visit on Willard Clifton. Malcom told me he was holding up all shipments of army payrolls until I had a chance to look things over.''

''You may already be too late, Mr. Slocum,'' Dawson said. ''A train left San Antone late last night with a payroll bound for Fort Davis. But the army put ten guards on that train, an' they wasn't green kids who'd just signed on for a hitch. Some gent by the name of Cletus Huling was in the baggage car too, some sort of detective from Kansas City.''

''I know Cletus Huling,'' Slocum said, taking a deep pull on his cigar after he said it. ''Huling is a part-time bounty hunter an' he has done some work for the Pinkertons.''

''I met him yesterday,'' Dawson said. ''Mean-lookin' bastard, with a shotgun an' two pistols. Big handlebar mustache an' has a real high opinion of how good he is with a gun.''

''I reckon he's good enough,'' Slocum said, feeling otherwise, although he didn't mention it.

''The payroll bound for Fort Davis an' then on to El Paso is nearly six thousand dollars. That's enough to tempt Frank Clanton to pull one of his jobs. I tried to warn Willard that it was bad business, only he wouldn't listen to me. He said this Cletus Huling could handle things.''

''Maybe he can,'' Slocum said aloud. Malcom had not made any mention of hiring another private detective. ''Did Willard Clifton say why Cletus was on this particular train?''

''Said he'd arranged for it himself, on account of how big the payroll was. He acted like them soldiers an' Mr. Huling was gonna take care of the problem the Texas an' Pacific has been havin' with Clanton.''

''What time did the train leave?'' Slocum asked, noticing that Rose Miller was standing at the bar with a glass of red wine in her hand, watching him, taking no pains to hide the fact that she was staring at him.

''Around midnight.''

''When will the train reach Devil's River Canyon?''

Dawson frowned. ''Hard to say. Maybe round midnight or early tomorrow mornin'.''

''Then if Frank Clanton knows about the payroll on board, he'll be there and it's too late to do anything about a robbery, if that's what he plans to do.''

''Mr. Clifton felt real sure Cletus Huling an' them soldiers could put a stop to it. I talked to him yesterday an' he sounded real sure about it.''

Slocum shrugged, looking back at Rose Miller in a way most women understood. "Not much I can do now," he told the sheriff as his glass of brandy arrived. He took the snifter and raised it while he stared at Rose, a salute of sorts to let her know he was aware she was looking at him.

He downed a swallow of brandy and spoke to the bartender. "Send the lady standing at the bar a drink. Whatever she wants in the way of fine wine. Tell her it came from me, with my compliments."

"She'll likely refuse it, mister," the barman said. "She ain't in the habit of takin' drinks from strangers."

Slocum smiled. "I hadn't planned on being a stranger to her much longer. Just take her a glass of your best French wine an' tell her it's with my compliments."

"Whatever you say," the barkeep replied, turning away with a five-dollar gold piece Slocum gave him.

Sheriff Dawson was reading Slocum's face. "You aim to get to know her?"

He nodded. "If she's tied in with this Frank Clanton, then it's a starting place. If she'll give me a chance to talk to her, she might tell me more than she intends to say. If I'm any judge of character, she's smart, and she knows she's pretty. I'll play that up some."

"But what about talkin' to Willard Clifton and Mr. Herring over at the bank?"

"I can do that tomorrow. I didn't know an army payroll had already left San Antone for Devil's River Canyon. If Clanton has a robbery planned, it's too late to do anything about it now. I have a chance of finding out if there's a connection between Rose and Clanton, and if I get lucky I might get some of that information tonight."

"She's a real uppity type. She may not even talk to you at all."

"I'll take that chance," he told the sheriff. "I'll know

in a minute or two, if she accepts the wine I'm sending her.''

Sheriff Dawson shook his head. ''I was told you was a real slick operator, Mr. Slocum, an' that you was 'bout as good with a gun as a man gets. Didn't know you went about railroad business this way.''

''I do things the easiest way, Sheriff Dawson,'' he replied as the bartender started toward Rose Miller with a long-stemmed glass of wine.

''Then I reckon I'll leave you till tomorrow mornin','' the lawman said, pushing back his chair. ''Good luck tryin' to meet Rose, only I don't figure you stand hardly no chance at all.''

2

Frank Clanton held a tight rein on his bay horse as the big locomotive came in sight. He spoke to Lefty Sikes. "That rail had better be loose enough to wreck this train."

"It's loose enough," Lefty replied. "I saw to pullin' them spikes myself."

"We'll miss a six-thousand-dollar payday if you're wrong about it."

"I ain't wrong. That steamer's gonna roll over like a kid's top off the side of that pass yonder. With a full head of steam it can't miss wreckin' every car hitched to it."

"Good," Clanton muttered. "That goddamn bounty hunter Cletus Huling's on the train, along with a bunch of soldiers. I hope the wreck kills every damn one of 'em." Frank ran a gloved hand across his beard stubble. The information he had on this train was accurate because he was sure of the source, and it meant they could lay low over in Mexico for a while. But the news that Cletus Huling was on the train hadn't been good, for Huling could be a dangerous man if he caught you just right, when he had the advantage. Huling was from Missouri, Clay County, a place infamous for the James gang and their cousins, the Younger brothers. Some said Huling was a distant relative of the Younger clan.

A rider with his face hidden behind a bandanna urged his horse up to Frank's. He spoke in a muffled voice. "We got four men on the other side, Boss. Gave 'em orders to keep their eyes on the baggage car, like you said."

"Shoot every son of a bitch who shows his face out of that car," Frank told Bob Walls, one of his most trusted men. "Be damn sure Cletus Huling don't slip off someplace when the train goes over. He's a slippery bastard, an' I've got a personal score to settle with him. He put a friend of mine in a grave in Abilene. Collected a three-hundred-dollar reward. I want every man in this outfit to make damn sure Huling is dead before we open that safe an' take off for Mexico. I'll pay an extra fifty dollars for his head."

"He's as good as dead now," Lefty said. "Fast as that train is movin', the crash is surely gonna kill him. But if it don't, I'm gonna see to killin' him myself."

"I told everybody," Bob added. "They all know what Huling looks like an' that he'll be in the baggage car. If he lives through the derailin', we'll blast him all to hell with our guns."

Frank was satisfied. "This'll be our last job for a spell, boys. With six thousand to split up, we can lay low for a few months . . . maybe longer. They'll quit expectin' us to hit a train here in Devil's River Canyon, figurin' we've moved west or damn near any other place. After things cool down, we'll hit 'em again, soon as I learn when there's another payroll on board."

Lefty chuckled. "The army sure has been good to us, Frank. We oughta send 'em a wire from down in Piedras Negras, tellin' 'em how much we appreciate the money."

"Might do just that," Frank said, watching a dark locomotive chug around a bend in Devil's River Canyon, its lone front lamp casting a golden glow over the dark tracks before it. "Maybe we can send 'em a jug of tequila."

Bob laughed. "No sense wastin' good agave squeeze on a damn soldier, Boss. Let's just send 'em that wire you was talkin' about."

Now Frank could hear the soft hiss of steam coming from the locomotive's boiler and valves. The chugging of steam pistons and the smokestack grew louder. "Like pretty music, ain't it, the sound made by a train?"

" 'Specially if it's carryin' an army payroll," Lefty said, reaching for his pistol. "Won't be long now till we're countin' all that money."

"We ain't got it counted out yet," Bob said with a note of doubt. "Last time we damn near didn't have enough dynamite to blow that safe."

"We've got enough this time," Frank assured him. "Liable to blow up the whole side of this canyon when we light the fuse on it."

"Tommy Lee said we had enough to blow up half of San Antone this time," Lefty remembered.

"I don't believe in takin' no chances," Frank said as the speeding train came down a gentle grade where a narrow wooden bridge crossed over a dry creek bed. "But don't forget Cletus Huling is guardin' that shipment. He ain't no tinhorn when it comes to lookin' out for money."

"A bullet in the right spot kills the toughest sons of bitches there is," Bob added. "When I shot ol' Sam Taggert, everybody said couldn't nobody kill him on account of he had a good-luck charm. That four-leaf clover didn't do Sam no good when I shot him just right."

Frank glanced over his shoulder. The rest of his men sat their horses with guns drawn, ready for the order to ride up to the train once it left the tracks. He looked at Lefty again, a narrowing of his eyelids changing his expression. "Just hope them rails come apart like they's supposed to. If things go like we planned, it won't take but a few minutes to kill them guards that make it out alive, if there is any. Then we blow the safe, sack up our money, an' ride like hell for Mexico."

"I can already taste tequila," Bob said. "I'm gonna buy me the prettiest *señorita* they've got an' lay between her legs fer a whole damn week."

Frank wasn't listening, watching the train, counting money in his head. "I'm gonna piss on Cletus Huling's face when we find his body in that wreck, or after somebody kills him. I owe him for what he done to Skeeter Munroe. Goddamn bounty hunter shot Skeeter in the back over three hundred dollars in reward money."

"Look yonder," Lefty said through his bandanna. "Ain't but one passenger car. Rest is boxcars. Won't be too many folks git killed this time so there won't be such a stink in the damn newspapers."

Frank was only concerned with the baggage car coupled right behind the coal tender. It was sure to jump the tracks when the locomotive and coal car went. During their second robbery here in Devil's River Canyon the locomotive's boiler had exploded, making a frightful noise, spooking the hell out of their horses. The engineer and brakeman had been cooked beyond recognition in the fire, a fire that almost reached the baggage car before the safe could be blown. Dozens of passengers were hurt or killed, some being consumed by flames as they stumbled about near the wreckage in a daze with their clothing on fire. It hadn't been a pretty sight to watch.

"Any time now," Lefty said, his gaze fixed on the section of rails where one track was loose.

A few seconds later Frank heard a mighty clatter, then the grinding of metal against metal as the locomotive swerved. A shower of sparks flew from the engine's wheels as it turned to the right. The coal tender jackknifed to the left, jerking the baggage car off the tracks. The crack of bending iron became a rolling, swelling wall of deafening noise.

Boxcars jumped the tracks as the nine-car train began to fold, cars ramming together, twisting, splintering, careening in different directions amid the crashing sounds. The giant engine tilted when it left the tracks completely, being pushed over on its side by the weight of oncoming cars behind it. The baggage car uncoupled from the tender, bouncing down a slight incline by the roadbed where tracks had been laid. A lone boxcar remained coupled to the rear of the baggage car, swaying, rocking back and forth, until it came loose, crashing into a thicket of mesquite trees before the baggage car plunged into a dry streambed, grinding to a sudden halt.

The locomotive's boiler ruptured, sending a huge cloud of steam curling into the night sky. The caboose was the last car to topple off the tracks. A trainman jumped from the rear platform just as the caboose crunched into the wreckage of the passenger car. Frank could hear passengers screaming above the roar of escaping steam and grinding metal.

"Let's ride!" Frank shouted, spurring his nervous horse to a run, leading a charge toward the mangled train and the baggage car resting at the bottom of the shallow ravine.

In the light from a pale half-moon Frank saw two uniformed soldiers drop out of a crumpled door on the baggage car. One of them staggered a few steps and fell down flat. The other soldier bent over to help his companion, then heard the rumble of hoofbeats coming toward him. He reached for a holstered pistol and clawed it free, its metallic surface gleaming in the light from the night sky.

Lefty fired first, two quick shots from his Colt .44, and both went wide. Bob started shooting, one carefully aimed shot at a time, three gun blasts in a row.

The soldier stiffened.

"Got the son of a bitch!" Bob cried over the noise of so many running horses.

Frank wasn't thinking about soldiers. His mind was on the bounty hunter. He would be their most dangerous adversary if he'd survived the train wreck.

Guns began blasting from the far side of the tracks, so many they made a constant crackle, blossoming muzzle flashes brightening up the darkness on the other side of the train.

Where's Huling? Frank wondered, reining his galloping

horse straight for the open baggage-car door.

A shootist from Kansas by the name of Carl Hardin spurred his horse past Frank's, riding a stolen Thoroughbred Remount stallion with plenty of early speed. He held a rifle to his shoulder and fired into the door of the baggage car, and even from a distance of several hundred yards, Frank heard someone shout in agony.

As the distance closed between Frank's gang and the train, a terrific explosion sent horses swerving, bounding away from the sight of a fireball rippling away from the overturned locomotive on the far side of the rails. Some highly flammable substance, probably the oil used on pistol sleeves and pushrods, illuminated the dark as if the sun was briefly at high noon.

And this moment gave Frank a glimpse of a shadowy figure jumping down from the ruined baggage car, leaving by a rear door where the car jutted up from the creek bed. The man wore a derby hat and a split-tail frock coat, and carried a short shotgun in his right fist.

"There's Cletus!" he bellowed above the dying echo of the explosion. "Kill the son of a bitch before he gets away from that train!"

Lefty pulled his horse to the left. "I'll git him fer you, Boss!" he cried. "Just leave the bastard to me."

Frank was doubtful that Lefty, or any one man, could make certain of Huling's demise. He turned his horse to follow Lefty toward the short wooden bridge where he'd seen the figure take off in a crouching run.

"I owe it to Skeeter," he growled, letting emotion get the best of him, for the moment forgetting about the rich payload in the baggage car safe.

Lefty fired a wild pistol shot at a fleeting shadow, and Frank knew he'd been right to see to killing Cletus Huling himself. He asked his horse for more speed, galloping recklessly over beds of loose rock and cactus.

Then Carl appeared again, racing in front of them with

his gun leveled between the stallion's ears. He saw a target Frank couldn't see. Seconds later, he fired.

Frank's horse tripped over something in the dark and went down on its chest, almost spilling him from the saddle. He spat a curse and dug his spurs into the gelding's sides.

The horse clambered to its feet and took off at a lope, one foreleg causing it pain when it felt weight. Frank did not care about his horse right then. His only mission was to make sure Cletus Huling was dead before they put a dynamite charge under the safe.

Light from the coal-oil explosion faded, and now everything was dark, brightened only by the partial moon.

"Where'd he go?" Frank demanded, stabbing sharp spur rowels into his injured horse's ribs.

His answer came from a dark spot near the bridge, when the thundering explosion of a shotgun gave off a muzzle flash. Carl Hardin was torn from the back of his mount as though he'd run into an invisible string of wire.

He tumbled off the rump of his stud and landed in a clump of cholla spines and broomweed, yelling for all he was worth while he was spinning through the air.

Frank's horse, despite its bad leg, bounded away from the sound of the shotgun.

Frank grabbed the saddlehorn just in time to keep from being spilled into the same tangle of thorns where Hardin had taken his fall.

"There he is!" a faraway voice shouted. "Kill him afore he gits to them bridge timbers."

The rattle of gunfire came from outlaws' guns on either side of the wrecked train. Bullets whined harmlessly through the air, and Frank Clanton knew they were in for a manhunt before the safe could be blasted. Somehow, Cletus Huling had gotten away.

3

Rose Miller daintily tilted her wineglass to her ruby lips and took a swallow. At first she had refused the glass of wine Slocum sent her with a simple gesture, waving it away with one hand. But when the bartender motioned to the table where Slocum sat, she glanced at him a moment, then smiled and accepted the drink before looking the other way.

"She's a haughty bitch," Slocum muttered to himself after the sheriff departed. He continued to stare at her, *wanting* her to know he was looking at her. She was a game-player, and he knew her type all too well. But he was just as sure he could have his way with her tonight if he persisted.

He stubbed out his cigar and sipped more brandy, waiting. The next move would also be his, although it had to be timed perfectly. Women like Rose were curious, like house cats, and Slocum understood how to bait her.

She was, he had to admit, extremely beautiful for a woman in a Texas town. Not that Texas women weren't pretty. But most women with her looks would head for places like San Francisco or Denver, or back East to New York, where they could catch a rich man for a suitor, or a husband.

He leaned back in his chair and pretended to be interested

17

in a poker game at a nearby table. If he appeared to be too eager to meet Rose, she would ignore him. But every now and then he would let his gaze pass across her face, hesitating briefly as though he'd seen something he liked. Almost every time, he caught her looking at him from the corner of her eye.

She'll come when I call her, just like a kitten, he thought. He'd met stiffer challenges than Rose Miller over the years, and he enjoyed seeing if he could lure her into his web, or more properly, his bed. It was a contest usually initiated by pretty women. Slocum liked the fact that he was sometimes able to turn the tables on them.

From very early manhood he'd been told that his rugged good looks were disturbing to certain kinds of women. His raven black hair and muscular frame worked like advertisements, under the right circumstances, and what dangled between his legs made him welcome to return to the bedrooms of women all across the West. It wasn't simply that he'd been born with a big cock. . . . over the years he'd learned how to use it correctly.

He waved the barkeep over and ordered another brandy, and then he said, "Invite the pretty blond lady at the bar to share a drink with me. Tell her my name's John Slocum, and I'd be honored to have her share company with me."

"She won't come," the bartender said.

Slocum intended to make Rose come in more ways than one, yet he merely said, "Ask her for me." He handed the man another coin and turned his attention back to the card game. The barman went over to Rose and whispered something in her ear.

"You're very brash," she said, a hint of a smile crossing her face. "What made you think I'd accept your offer?" She had allowed him to pull a chair back for her when she came to his table.

He returned to his seat and raised his glass. "I'm what you might call a gambler, only I seldom play with cards or dice. I gamble on certain women, only the most beautiful women, because I truly enjoy their company.''

"How bold of you,'' she said. "I almost refused. You take too much for granted, Mr. Slocum.''

"Please call me John.''

"Not quite yet, Mr. Slocum. Once again, you've assumed far too much.''

"Then so be it. I shall address you as Miss Miller and you may call me Mr. Slocum.''

"And how is it that you know my name?''

"Sheriff Dawson told me who you were. I'm sure you saw us sitting together earlier in the evening.''

"What makes you so certain I noticed you? And what business might you have with our sheriff? You are far too sure of yourself, Mr. Slocum. Some might call it arrogance.''

"I'm not arrogant. Interested in getting to know you is a better way to put it. My business with the sheriff is nothing of any importance. Someone stole my horse on the road from Austin and I only wanted to get it back.'' It wasn't true, of course, about the stolen horse, but he had to have a way to explain why he'd been talking to a peace officer. He couldn't tell her it was because she might be a key figure in a number of train robberies, or at the very least an information source for the holdup men in Devil's River Canyon.

Her deep blue eyes fell to the gun belted around his waist. "You are armed, Mr. Slocum. Why didn't you shoot this horse thief?''

"Never had the chance,'' he replied as the bartender brought Rose another glass of wine. "I was otherwise occupied.''

"Otherwise occupied? Do I dare ask for an explanation? Or would I be better off not knowing?''

"I was, in truth, in a young woman's bedroom.''

"Then you are a common scoundrel who beds any woman he happens to meet?''

"Not true, Miss Miller. I knew this particular lady quite well . . . well enough to be invited to share her bed."

She smiled again. "I see. So you make it a habit to travel from one woman's bed to another on your journeys?"

Slocum grinned. "When I get the chance, if the bedroom belongs to the right kind of woman."

"You are, indeed, nothing but a scoundrel. I wish now I had not accepted your invitation to sit at your table. Men like you are a dime a dozen."

"I deny being a scoundrel," he said, having fun with the bantering back and forth. "I might agree that I'm an opportunist at times. However, it must be the right opportunity."

"You are also quite vain, to believe you can pick and choose your opportunities with women," she said, feigning annoyance. "I can assure you that you'll have no such opportunity with me. I'm not a tramp."

"And I never implied that I could believe that about you. I am being falsely accused."

"Then why did you invite me over for a drink?"

"Merely to make your acquaintance, Miss Miller. It never once crossed my mind to take you to bed."

"You're a bad liar. I saw you looking at me . . . the *way* you looked at me."

"Simple admiration for rare beauty, my dear."

"Nonsense. It was lust I saw in your eyes."

"You've mistaken curiosity for lust. I knew at once you were a real lady, a woman of refinement who would be offended by ungentlemanly behavior."

Rose emptied her glass in two swallows, revealing a healthy capacity for liquor. She dabbed at her painted lips with a napkin. "At the risk of sounding unladylike, Mr. Slocum, I also recognize bullshit when I hear it."

"I never expected to hear a word like that come from your mouth. Under the circumstances, I suppose it's understandable, only you don't know me well enough to make a judgment like the one you've made. I'm being sincere with you."

"Horseshit," she said, saying it playfully. "Nothing you have said to me was sincere. You're only trying to take me to bed."

"That simply isn't true. May I buy you another glass of wine while I try to convince you of my honesty and sincerity?"

"Perhaps," Rose replied, lowering her voice while staring deeply into his eyes. "I'll think about it a moment, but I want you to understand that no matter how charming you may be, or how handsome you are, I won't be persuaded to take you to my bedroom upstairs. Make no mistake about it, Mr. Slocum."

"I'll order you another glass of wine," he said, raising his hand for the bartender. "As I told you before, the thought never crossed my mind . . ."

She ran her fingers over the full length of his prick as she guided it between the downy lips of her wet mound. "It's very big," she gasped, her full, naked body pressed hard against the mattress by his weight. "I'm not sure I can . . . take all of it inside me."

A small lantern on a nightstand next to the bed allowed him to see the rounded curves of her nakedness, the sheer perfection of it.

"I'll be gentle," he promised, pushing the head of his throbbing cock into her warm cunt, feeling moist resistance when the muscles in her creamy thighs tightened. She was panting now, digging her fingernails into his back. He held back on his first thrust, waiting for her to open.

"You tricked me," she gasped. "You gave me too much wine. I didn't want you to do this. You took unfair advantage of me with liquor."

"I was overcome by desire for a beautiful woman," he told her. "Can't blame me for that."

She parted her legs a bit more. "You're a rogue and a

scoundrel. I'm not the kind of woman who invites a man to her bed upon our first meeting. I don't know what's come over me. It *has* to be the wine."

Slocum shoved an inch of his rigid member into her honey pot, and the moment he did, she took in a sudden, deep breath. Her spine went rigid.

"Dear me!" she exclaimed. "It's much too large!"

"I said I'd be gentle."

She curled the backs of her legs around his and drew him closer, slightly deeper inside her cunt, reaching for his buttocks with both hands. "It does feel . . . good," she said with a sigh as she began to hunch against the thickness of his shaft. "Oh, it does feel so very good, even though it is much too large. I do not have much experience with men. I'm very selective about who I sleep with."

"I could tell that about you the moment I laid eyes on you tonight," he murmured, nuzzling one of her ample breasts, his tongue flicking over its twisted pink nipple. "I was doubtful I would ever get the chance to know you in . . . a personal way."

"It's the wine," she said, thrusting her pelvis so that his cock went deeper. "I would never have allowed this to happen without drinking too much wine."

He met her thrusts with movements of his own, shoving more of his prick gently inside her opening. He felt her shudder as her fingers dug into his flesh.

"That . . . hurts," Rose whimpered. Yet she kept on hunching in a rhythmic, demanding way, her eyelids screwed shut. Sweat beaded on her skin despite the coolness of her room above the Velvet Slipper on a late fall evening with the windows open, curtains fluttering in a breeze.

Downstairs, the music from an old upright piano had stopped, and Slocum knew the hour was late, that the saloon was closed for the night. It had been well after midnight before Rose invited him up, after eight or nine glasses of red wine.

"You don't really want me to stop, do you?" he asked, for he was sure he knew the answer.

"No," she gasped. "Not . . . now. It does . . . hurt, but in a nice . . . way."

He pushed a fraction more of his cock into her, feeling his balls rise.

Tremors shook her limbs, and her breathing came in short, rapid pants. "Harder," she said in a hoarse whisper, "but not too hard."

He obliged her, driving his blood-engorged member farther, with more force, thrusting with greater speed.

"Oh, John!" she cried, and suddenly her entire body turned to iron, her legs straightening, fingers clawing into his ass until he was sure they drew blood.

His own climax came quickly when her internal muscles tightened around him. He let out a groan, a groan of pure pleasure as his jism exploded into her womb.

"Please! Please!" she moaned, caught in a wave of ecstasy while he continued to stab his prick into the beautiful blond woman. Her spine formed an arch and her heels dug into the mattress. Rose clamped her teeth together, her face twisted in release.

Moments later she collapsed underneath him, wheezing, trying to catch her breath. The last of his seed leaked from his cock, and then he too lay still in her arms.

For a time he listened to her rapid breathing, feeling the beating of her heart. He kissed her cheek gently and stroked her damp hair.

"That was nice," he said softly.

"It was wonderful," she told him, unwilling to take her arms from his neck. "I've . . . never had it happen . . . so fast. You made me come so quickly."

"Maybe it was the wine," he said, half joking.

She shook her head on the pillow. "It's the size of that magnificent cock, Mr. Slocum."

He grinned. "I couldn't make all of it fit," he told her in a teasing way, although it was the truth.

"Maybe we can try again," she replied.

He fondled one nipple, rubbing it between his thumb and forefinger. "You'll get no argument out of me."

4

"Yonder he is!" a voice cried.

Frank swung his horse toward the yell, feeling the animal flounder underneath him. He would need another horse to make it away from the train after they got the money, for his bay was too badly crippled from its fall and it stood no chance of making it to the border.

A pistol cracked on the far side of the tracks near the railroad bridge. Seconds later, the shot was answered by the roar of a shotgun, echoing off rocky cliffs where the train lay in pieces, twisted wreckage everywhere, flames licking up the sides of the overturned locomotive, giving off an eerie yellow light.

"You bastard!" Frank hissed, clamping his jaw, knowing the shotgun had been fired by Cletus Huling at one of his men hidden in brush beyond the rails. For the moment he forgot about the army payroll in the baggage car safe. He decided it was worth a bit of extra time to make damn sure Huling was killed. If he could, he meant to do it himself.

He rode past the pellet-riddled body of Carl Hardin and gave it no thought, other than a slight touch of regret that one of his men wouldn't make it to Mexico. These were the risks of the train-robbing profession, something his men should have understood by now.

"I see him!" a high-pitched voice shouted. "He's next to that bridge support over—"

A thundering explosion ended Jimmy Ballard's warning before he got it all said as Huling took aim with his scattergun and fired.

Now, more determined than ever to see to Huling's demise, Frank spurred his laboring mount directly toward the bridge. He saw a horseman dash past the wrecked passenger car with a pistol aimed in front of him.

"Soldiers! Soldiers!" someone bellowed from the ravine where the baggage car had come to rest. Frank glanced over his left shoulder.

Five men in dark uniforms came spilling from the baggage car with rifles in their hands. Frank's hopes that the derailment would kill or seriously injure most of the army guards watching the payroll were quickly dashed. He'd been warned that these were seasoned veterans riding this train, not green recruits as so often in the past when he'd hit other trains from San Antonio.

A rifle barked somewhere near the locomotive, and one of the soldiers went down in a heap. A second shot was just as successful, sending a uniformed man sprawling on the ravine bottom as his rifle fell from his hands.

Then a pistol went off, four shots fired as quickly as a revolver could shoot, and one more soldier slumped out of sight in the darkness.

Frank returned his attention back to the bridge where he'd last seen the bounty hunter. His horse was barely able to hold a gallop as he came within less than a hundred yards of the bridge supports.

In an instant when the light and shadow was just right, he saw a shape move near one of the timbers. He cocked his Colt and fired too early, then waited until his horse brought him closer to the movement he'd glimpsed, the outline of a man. His horse almost fell when it crossed loose stones, and yet he continued to spur it relentlessly, caring nothing for the animal, his only thought to end Cletus Huling's life at any cost.

A blossom of bright light flared underneath the bridge and his bay tumbled to the ground. Shotgun pellets ripped tiny holes in Frank's left shirtsleeve and tore off his hat, a few stinging his cheeks as he was thrown over the downed horse's neck.

He landed with a grunt in yucca spines and thorny brush, and ignored the pain from his fall and the minor shotgun wounds, to scramble to his feet with his pistol clamped in his fist. He was stunned momentarily from the fall, and unable to locate the right bridge support where he'd seen Huling and the muzzle flash.

From the east a six-gun spat flame, popping, sending a stabbing finger of orange-yellow light toward the bridge. And then a scream of anguish followed, when a man staggered away from one of the timbers with both hands pressed to his stomach.

"I got him!" Bob Walls cried.

Frank let out a sigh and lowered his pistol even as another gun battle raged near the baggage car. He watched Cletus Huling sway and stumble a few steps more, until a man on a horse rode up to him and fired at the bounty hunter's head.

Huling whirled, jolted by that bullet's impact, then went down on his knees as if he meant to pray.

"Atta boy, Bob!" Frank shouted, a twisted grin lifting the corners of his mouth.

The bounty hunter fell over on his chest and lay still, just as Bob jerked his horse to a full stop. "He's a dead son of a bitch, Boss! You ain't never seen so much blood!"

Frank's attention returned to the money. "Get over to that baggage car an' help 'em kill the rest of them soldiers. I've gotta find me a horse someplace."

Bob trotted his horse over to Frank, smoke still curling from his revolver. "Carl ain't gonna be needin' his no more. In case you didn't know, Huling gunned him down.''

"I saw it," Frank said. "Go help the rest of the boys an' then let's set that dynamite."

"You want me to fetch you Carl's horse?"

"Not just yet. I'm gonna walk over yonder an' look right close at Cletus . . . just to make goddamn sure the sumbitch is dead as nails."

"I shot him square in the face, Boss."

"Get goin'. I'm gonna make sure."

Frank trudged over to the railroad bridge and looked down at what was left of Cletus Huling's head. Bob's shot had gone plumb through the bounty hunter's skull, being as it was fired at such close range.

"I hope the goddamn worms eat you," Frank spat at the still corpse. "You got just what you deserved, bounty-huntin' asshole. . . ."

The explosion sent the roof of the baggage car skyward in a thousand swirling pieces. As the noise died down, they could hear bits of sheet metal and wood pattering to the ground all around the train wreck. In a moment of silence that followed, Frank heard a passenger whimpering some-where in the darkness, the voice of a woman crying.

"Get the money loaded!" Frank snapped, sending Lefty and Bob and Cotton Polk rushing toward the ruined bag-gage car with canvas bags. Cotton's brother, Raymond, held their horses, attempting to settle the terrified animals after the huge explosion. One side of the baggage car had been blown to bits, while the other had somehow remained upright.

"Sure hope that safe door got blowed off," Raymond said in his typically matter-of-fact way. Nothing ever seemed to excite Raymond Polk, not even counting money.

"You can bet on it," Frank replied. "That was enough dynamite to blow this whole train to hell."

"Counted ten dead soldiers, Boss, an' Bob said he killed that bounty hunter. Both trainmen is dead. Ain't seen no sign of the conductor, but I don't figure he'll give us no problems now.''

Frank wondered idly how many passengers had been killed in the derailment. "It was one hell of a wreck, Raymond. An' we just made ourselves one helluva payday.''

Raymond glanced over his shoulder at the night around them. "Never was one to worry too much, Boss, but the Texas an' Pacific ain't likely to stand for no more of this. Next time they'll hire a whole army of bounty hunters, men who know how to shoot, an' we'll be goin' up against some bigger numbers, the way I got it figured. We hit this railroad mighty hard in the pocketbook. They won't make it this easy fer us again.''

Frank nodded, for he'd been thinking the same thing himself for months. "That's how come this is our last job for a spell, Raymond. We'll have more'n enough to last us down in Piedras Negras for maybe a year.''

"If there's really six thousand in that safe,'' Raymond said as though he doubted it. "That'd be our biggest haul since we took up robbin' trains.''

"There'll be six thousand,'' Frank told him. "My source ain't been wrong about the money yet. Six thousand was just too temptin' to pass up.''

"It's damn sure a bunch of money,'' Raymond agreed. "Lefty said Bob got that bounty hunter. I reckon that's how come he was on this train in the first place, on account of it was so much loot this time.''

Frank nodded again. "When I first heard it was six thousand I figured the railroad was baitin' us, like they aimed to set a trap in this canyon some place. But we scouted the whole damn river an' there wasn't nobody. The railroad had to believe that havin' Cletus Huling on board, along with so many soldiers, was enough to handle us. We damn sure proved 'em wrong.''

"Too bad about Carl,'' Raymond said as he saw Cotton jump down with bags of money in each fist. "He was a good man to have sidin' with us.''

"His luck ran out," Frank said.

"Jimmy's hurt bad. Bleedin' from a hundred holes when Huling shot him. He may not make it. Wilson had to help him climb on his horse."

Frank recalled hearing Jimmy Ballard scream when Huling shot in the direction of his voice. "He'll have to stay in the saddle by his lonesome," Frank said. "We gotta get to the border quick as we can. Ain't got time to nurse him along." Lefty and Bob followed Cotton out of the ruined railroad car carrying more bags of loot.

"Seems kinda cold, Frank, not to help Jimmy. He's been with us right from the beginnin'."

"Every man in this outfit knows the chances we're takin'. I ain't bein' cold about it, just practical. We can't slow down for just one man who's hurt. Mexico is the only place where we'll be safe and Jimmy knowed it. When a man eats lead in this business, it comes with the job sometimes."

"Sure wish it hadn't been Jimmy," Raymond said.

Frank gave him a cold stare. "You'd rather it'd been you, Raymond? Or your little brother?"

"Never said that, Boss. Just said it was a shame to leave him if he can't ride."

Lefty was the first to reach the horses. He had four sacks stuffed with currency, two in each hand. "You shoulda seen what that dynamite done!" he cried, handing bags up to Raymond and Wilson Giles. "Some of the banknotes got burnt, but hell, you ain't never seen so much cash in all your life."

Bob gave four sacks to Sonny Jones to tie across his saddle while Cotton trotted over to Clyde Devers with three bulging bags of bills. Frank had turned to mount Carl Hardin's horse when he saw Josh Walker riding toward them leading Jimmy Ballard on his pinto, slumped over the pommel of his saddle.

Frank got aboard the stallion, gathering his reins just as Josh and Jimmy rode up.

"He's bad hurt, Mr. Clanton," Josh said, aiming a thumb over his shoulder at Jimmy. "Bleedin' like a stuck hog."

"Bring him along, just so he can stay in the saddle. If he falls off, we gotta leave him." He gave the men around him a hard stare. "You boys know it can't be no other way. One man can't be the cause of the rest of us gettin' caught. Now let's ride!"

Men turned their horses away from the train, forming a line single file across a stretch of limestone behind Frank, thus to leave as few tracks as possible for the law, or the army, to find when they came to investigate. The train wouldn't be reported missing until sometime tomorrow, when it didn't arrive at the water stop at Pandale. Even then, a rider would have to be sent to old Fort Stockton, an abandoned army post where a few cowmen and goat ranchers lived, in order to send a telegram to San Antonio to inform the railroad office that the train had failed to show up.

"I got it figured there's more than six thousand here," Lefty said. "Damn, you never seen so much money."

"We'll count it tomorrow mornin' after we cross the Rio Grande," Frank explained.

"Can't believe we're so rich."

Frank scowled at the dark canyon, heading for an old Comanche Indian trail they followed to leave the Devil's River area. "We ain't got to Mexico yet," he warned. "Keep your eyes open an' your mouth shut, just in case we missed an army patrol when we scouted this canyon before sundown."

"We'd have knowed it if soldiers was here," Bob said as he rode behind Lefty.

"I sure as hell hope you're right," Frank said.

"Hold up a minute!" Josh said at the rear of the procession. "Jimmy can't sit this horse no longer. I been holdin' him up fer a spell, only he's out cold now."

"Push him off an' keep his horse," Frank ordered, raising his voice more than he wanted so Josh could hear him. "Take his guns before he falls."

"Sure seems cold," Raymond Polk muttered again as the thud of a body sounded from the darkness behind them.

5

"Tell me why you came to San Antonio," Rose asked, tracing her fingertip over the hair on his chest, lying beside him with the lamp turned down low.

"To visit a friend."

Her naked body was still moist from their lovemaking, and he admired her gentle curves, the swirls of golden hair sprouting from her mound, her flawless skin, and the depth of her sparkling blue eyes giving off a curious radiance despite the darkness cloaking her bedroom.

"What does your friend do?" she asked, smiling, running her hand down the muscles of his back.

"He's in the railroad business," Slocum said, and at the word "railroad," a change came over her face. "Not really a friend . . . he's a friend of a friend, so to speak. The company has an office here."

"You must be talking about someone with the Texas and Pacific Company," she said, a note of caution creeping into her voice. "Downstairs, you told me you were in the race-horse business."

He nodded, sensing he was already getting more than he had hoped for so soon. "I sell prize horses . . . thoroughbreds, to top breeders in several states and western territories. I've sold a number of good stallions to Malcom

33

Warren, vice president of the Texas and Pacific. Malcom and I have known each other for years. It was at his suggestion that I came to San Antone, to make the acquaintance of a man named Willard Clifton. Mr. Clifton is the local manager for the Texas and Pacific freight office. Apparently, Mr. Clifton also has an eye for good horseflesh. He has expressed an interest in investing in some blooded breeding stock to begin raising his own racehorses.''

Rose wasn't completely convinced yet. "But what does this have to do with your meeting with Sheriff Dawson?"

He kissed her cheek lightly and smiled. "I'm not all that fond of talking to a lawman myself, but as I told you, someone stole my horse on the road from Austin. Also, Malcom told me there had been some trouble with train wrecks west of here, and that if I intended to ship any blooded horses down from Denver, I'd be better off talking to Sheriff Dawson first. Some of the trains have been robbed, Malcom said.''

"Train robberies?"

"That's what Malcom told me. He said to be sure I didn't put good horses on a train carrying any army payroll money out west, because some of his trains have been derailed and robbed of army payrolls. Malcom advised me to ask the sheriff here when it would be safest to send a few horses by rail.''

"Then you don't know Willard . . . Mr. Clifton?"

"Never met him. I was to make my introductions tomorrow morning and ask about the schedule down from Denver, in case he should be interested in some racing bloodlines I'm offering for sale. Malcom told me he'd sent a letter of introduction down, so Mr. Clifton could talk freely with me about the . . . train problems he's been having." It was part truth. Malcom Warren had sent a letter to Clifton, simply an introduction and a brief mention of Slocum's racing stock. Malcom hadn't come right out and said so, but it was clear he suspected that Willard Clifton might be the source of information regarding the army payroll shipments handled by the Texas and Pacific. Slocum decided to press her, but not too much. "Do you know this Willard Clifton, by chance?"

She regarded him warily. "I'm acquainted with him. However, I don't know him well at all. Why do you ask?"

"I suppose I'm wondering what sort of fellow he is. Malcom didn't tell me much about him . . . only that he showed an interest in owning good thoroughbreds. I like to know the kind of man I'm dealing with. I won't sell good horses to someone who'd mistreat them, or to some fool who knows nothing about bloodlines and how to increase the chances of producing a good foal. It would be a waste of top breeding stock to sell them to someone who knows nothing about the business. Raising winning racehorses requires a great deal of careful study when it comes to matching the right mare with the proper stallion."

"Then you're really a horse dealer?"

"That's my trade. I've done other things. There was the war, and for several years afterward I drifted around from one place to another."

Rose seemed to relax somewhat, yet she was still wary. "You said your horse was stolen on the road down from Austin . . . while you were in a woman's bedroom. It would seem you care more about women than your horses."

"It does sound strange, I'll admit. The woman provided a powerful distraction."

Her eyes locked on his. "And am I a distraction, Mr. John Slocum?"

"Indeed you are."

"This young woman . . . was she pretty?"

"Very pretty. But not nearly as beautiful as you, my dear, and I mean that sincerely."

"I have a feeling you've said that often, to any number of girls."

He wagged his head emphatically. "I protest my innocence, dear lady. I rarely ever tell a woman she is beautiful.

There is a difference between being pretty and true beauty. You, Rose Miller, are a natural beauty.''

She kissed him. ''Make love to me,'' she whispered, ''only this time, please do it gently no matter what I say in the heat of the moment.''

''Are you blaming me for being too rough with you?''

''Not exactly. It's hard to put into words. It felt so good at the time that I wanted more of you.''

''And now you want less?''

She giggled. ''Not any less, perhaps, but I do wish you would be gentler.''

She chewed his earlobe, biting it gently.

Slocum nibbled her taut pink nipple, flicking the end of his tongue over it.

''I don't think I can take it . . . again,'' Rose whispered. ''I'm a little sore.'' Warm air from her lips brushed his neck while she spoke.

He removed his mouth from her breast. ''You told me the truth when you said you weren't very experienced with men. I like that in a woman.''

''I'm choosy.''

''As you should be, Rose. You are a truly beautiful woman who can pick and choose the men she wants and the men she does not want. But I'm certain you already know that. A beautiful woman doesn't have to be told she's beautiful . . . the attention of so many men convinces her.''

She reached for his swelling cock, moving her dainty hand up and down his girth. ''You seem to know a great deal about women, John.''

''I've known a few.''

''You are very sure of yourself.''

''I hadn't thought about it really.''

''That is very appealing to a woman, when a man is sure of his manhood.''

''I reckon I do what comes naturally. I can't say as I ever thought about it.''

Her hand was moving faster, jacking up and down his shaft as her breathing quickened. "You have a certain . . . charm. I can't quite put my finger on it."

"Maybe you have your fingers around it, Rose?" he said with a grin.

"That's not what I mean, although you *are* quite a man in that regard."

Slocum ran his forefinger between the lips of her cunt, and when he felt dampness, he rolled between her thighs. "This time it'll be different," he promised. "It won't hurt at all. You should trust me."

"I don't trust any men," she said, mocking him by the way she said it.

"Too bad. You should learn how." While her hand continued to stroke his prick, he steered the head of his member to the lips of her cunt, parting them gently when he applied a slight bit of pressure.

"Men have always lied to me," she said softly, lifting her pelvis to meet his organ, her pupils dilating with the anticipation of pleasure. Her breathing became even faster. "In the beginning, when I was a young girl, I trusted men. They all betrayed me, one way or another. I've been looking for an honest man ever since, and I've come to believe that they do not exist at all."

"It's too narrow a view," he protested, pushing his cock until her lips opened for him. "You must not give up, for the world has a great many honest men.

"I've had . . . bad experiences," she said with a sigh, closing her eyes when she felt him begin to enter her.

"I hope you won't feel this evening is one of them," he told her as her limbs started to tremble with desire.

Rose dug her fingernails into the small of his back. "Not this part," she whispered next to his ear. "This part has been very good."

"But you don't trust me."

"No," she moaned, moving her head side to side on the

pillow when more of his cock penetrated her, though her eyes remained closed.

"Simply because I'm a man?"

"Stop talking, John. I want you to make me feel good and stop all this talking."

Her cunt opened a tiny bit more, and he took advantage of opportunity, inching more of his shaft into the warm, wet tunnel of her womanhood.

"Yes," she hissed, gritting her teeth. "That's what I want from you."

Rose ground her abdomen against his belly, moving in small circles, rotating her hips on the bedsheet while she tightened her embrace, drawing him to her.

Slocum planted his mouth over hers, kissing her deeply as a moan of pure desire escaped from her throat. As her passion mounted, her thrusting increased, and more of his cock went easily into her opening.

Bedsprings began to squeak as they rocked back and forth on the mattress. Slocum gripped the headboard with both hands to add power to his driving prick, yet he found he was still unable to enter her fully, completely.

Rose twisted her face away from his kiss to gasp for air. "Harder," she said, a plea in her voice.

"You asked me to be gentle."

"Forget what I said. Do it harder."

"You won't be angry?"

"Please . . . do it harder. Faster."

He was more than willing to grant her request, and with a powerful push he slammed two more inches of his stiff prick inside her.

"Yes! Yes!" she cried, shivering, though her body was now drenched with perspiration. Rose wound her legs around the backs of his thighs, digging her heels into his calves.

He felt the tips of her painted fingernails eating into his flesh, and he ignored the pain. His back and buttocks bore a number of similar scars from other nights spent like this.

Rose was one of the most passionate women he'd ever bedded, and she was certainly one of the most beautiful.

The headboard was tapping the bedroom wall with each drive he made inside her, and the squeaking of bedsprings grew even louder as Rose neared her climax. Her nostrils flared each time she took a quick breath, and her mouth was open as if she feared she might suffocate.

When he felt her internal muscles quiver, he buried the full length of his thick shaft in her mound, and the moment he did he heard her scream.

"Now! Oh, please!"

Her cry would be enough to awaken everyone on the second floor of the Velvet Slipper, but at the moment he did not care who else knew Rose was enjoying herself. His testicles lifted while a warm sensation spread through his groin.

With a ferocity he hadn't expected, Rose hammered her cunt against the base of his shaft, and suddenly she went completely rigid underneath him, groaning while he kept on thrusting his prick in and out until at last, his balls released their load.

He too groaned when his climax came, and it was like a river had broken through an earthen dam. His seed flowed into her endlessly, or so it seemed. Finally, he relaxed and let his full weight rest atop her sweating body.

For several seconds Rose was unable to speak, sucking in more air, a faint wheezing sound coming from deep inside her chest. Slocum's cock softened. As they lay locked together, their sweat mingled, soaking the sheets and pillowcase.

"Oh, dear John," she managed to gasp, when her breathing slowed somewhat. "That was . . . the biggest one . . . I ever had. I thought it would last forever."

"The biggest cock?" he asked innocently, although he was sure he knew the answer.

"No, darling. The biggest release. I didn't know they could . . . last so long."

Slocum wanted more information from her, not related to her climaxes, but about Willard Clifton and an outlaw named Frank Clanton and how Clanton knew when an army payroll was aboard a certain train. He kissed her cheek. This wasn't the right time to ask.

6

The railroad depot in San Antonio was a sprawling affair, a brick passenger platform and rows of shaded benches beneath the roof of a porch running the length of the ticket windows, then a waiting room, and beyond this building rows of freight company offices fronted by loading docks. The Southern Pacific had its own office, as did the Cotton Belt. Last in line was the Texas and Pacific. Behind a glass-paned door, Slocum found a young clerk seated behind a desk shuffling through a stack of papers. Another office was attached to the first, and its door was open to allow scant breezes to flow through open windows.

The boy looked up when Slocum came in. "May I help you, sir?"

"I'm here to see Mr. Willard Clifton. Tell him John Slocum is calling. He should have a letter of introduction from Malcom Warren regarding my arrival."

"Yessir," the clerk said, almost jumping out of his chair when he heard Warren's name. It was obvious the vice president of operations was well known to him.

The boy disappeared into the rear office. Moments later he came out. "Please go in, Mr. Slocum. Mr. Clifton has been expecting you."

Slocum entered the back office, to find a chubby man

with a pallid complexion and fleshy jowls, dressed in a vest and white shirt. He appeared to be in his forties, with thinning brown hair combed and oiled flat against his skull. He got up and extended his hand. "I've been looking forward to this, Mr. Slocum. I'm Willard Clifton. Please take a chair."

Slocum shook with Clifton, and took a straight-backed wooden chair opposite a cluttered desk. "Malcom has told me a great deal about you, Mr. Clifton. You are one of his most valuable managers."

"I'm flattered," Clifton said, returning to his swivel chair heavily, as though standing for any length of time required a lot of effort. A thin smile left his face. "As you may know, we've had a few problems lately. I'm sure Malcom must have mentioned it to you."

"The robberies," Slocum replied. "He did say something about them."

"Is that why you're here?" Clifton asked, and it seemed he had begun to perspire a little. "Mr. Warren's letter only said you'd be seeking information, and to give you my full cooperation at all times. He said you were a highly respected gentleman from Denver and a long-time friend. I assumed your visit must have something to do with the holdups."

"Not really. Malcom said you might be interested in some thoroughbred racehorses I own."

Clifton's face mirrored surprise, as Slocum had known it would. "He did? I'm not a horseman. Why, I only attended the races up in Fort Worth with Malcom on one or two occasions. I feel there must be some mistake."

"Malcom seemed sure of it when we exchanged telegrams a few weeks ago."

Clifton swallowed. "Perhaps I did express some interest in racing stock. However, I don't think I said anything about a wish to own some."

"A misunderstanding, possibly. However, I have other racehorse clients in South Texas, and in order to do business with them I'll have to ship stallions and mares by rail. Of course, being Malcom's friend, I'd use the Texas and Pacific Company exclusively.''

"Of course. It would be a pleasure to handle the shipping for you. I wish I could recall what it was I might have said that made Mr. Warren think I wanted to purchase race-horses. I feel sure—almost sure—that I made no mention of it while I was in Fort Worth.''

"It's of no importance. But I must be certain that the Texas and Pacific will be a safe way to ship livestock. Malcom told me there had been several serious derailments in which passengers and trainmen were killed.''

"I'm afraid it's true,'' Clifton said with a sigh, "although I've just taken measures to rectify the problem. I suppose Malcom told you that our trains carrying army payrolls west to frontier outposts have been robbed. Malcom has con-cluded, and I quite agree, that someone among the robbers has inside information as to when, and on what trains, these payrolls are carried. There's a stretch of track running through a particularly desolate area known as the Devil's River Canyon. All the robberies have occurred there, within a fifty-mile stretch of track. The cavalry has sent out patrols to search for traces of these clever holdup men, and they've found nothing. Even when our baggage cars containing the money are heavily guarded, somehow the robbers are able to defeat the guards, and a tragic number of soldiers have been killed or seriously wounded. This section of rail line is one of our main routes west. We simply can't allow these derail-ments and robberies to continue.''

"You mentioned some new measures you've taken?'' Slocum asked, even though he knew the details. It had to appear as if he did not know anything that he'd learned from the sheriff the previous night.

"I secured the services of a specialist in these matters,'' Clifton replied. ''He is a rather well-known detective and bounty hunter by the name of Cletus Huling. He is pres-ently aboard a train that left the night before last for El

Paso, passing through the Devil's River Canyon region. This train carries a rather large army payroll, guarded by ten soldiers in addition to Mr. Huling. The engineer was advised to proceed with caution through the canyon, watching closely for any objects placed upon the rails that might cause our locomotive to jump the tracks. All this should present the holdup men with a substantial obstacle if they somehow got word of our shipment.''

Slocum scowled as if deep in thought. ''How do you personally think the information regarding payrolls is being relayed to an outlaw band?''

Clifton evidenced exasperation, folding his hands across his vested belly. ''I wish the hell I knew. If this continues, it will most certainly cost me my job with the company. Mr. Warren is understandably concerned.''

''Could it be someone with the army fort here? Or do you suspect it comes from within the railroad itself?''

''I've examined every possibility. The young man out front has been questioned at length by gentlemen from our home office in Fort Worth, and by our local sheriff, Ike Dawson.'' Clifton lowered his voice. ''But the boy and his record withstands the closest scrutiny. He has no ties to men of bad character that we can find, and he has no money and no apparent motive. Our train crews do not know when a train contains valuable cargo until the last minute. Thus we can eliminate trainmen from any list of suspects. Frankly, I'm stumped, and so is the army post commander, General Davis. He insists he has thoroughly questioned all individuals at Fort Sam Houston who have any knowledge of the payroll disbursements. He too comes up with nothing.''

''This train that departed the night before last . . . has it made it through the canyon?''

''We don't know yet. Until it reaches a water and coal stop at Pandale, I have no way of finding out. There is no telegraph office at Pandale, but should the train not show up, our man operating the water station will ride to Fort

Stockton to wire us the news. In this case, so far, no news
is good news. When the train reaches Fort Stockton, the
conductor will wire us that all is well. We should be hearing
from Fort Stockton sometime later this morning, perhaps
as late as noon.''

"If the train arrives.''

"In either case,'' Clifton said. "I must admit I'm a bit
nervous about it.''

Slocum rested one leg across his knee, thinking. Clifton
did not appear to be hiding anything, and Slocum was a
pretty good judge of these things. He stared past Clifton
out an office window. "With ten soldiers and Cletus Huling
guarding the safe in the baggage car, it would take a fairly
large number of men to overpower them . . . unless they
dynamited the tracks or used some method to cause a serious wreck that would injure or kill some of the guards.''

"In the previous cases we haven't been able to be ab-
solutely sure how the derailments occurred,'' Clifton said.
"After the safe is dynamited open, so much damage is done
to nearby rails it is virtually impossible to discover what
was placed on the tracks to cause the locomotive to derail.''

"One time up near Denver this gang of robbers pulled
the spikes out of one rail so the train derailed the minute
the engine crossed it,'' Slocum said. He had been the one
who'd found out this rather important detail, but he wasn't
ready to reveal he'd done any detective work for a railroad
in the past. His presence in San Antonio needed to appear
to be related to his horse-breeding business, at least until
he learned who had gotten information about the army payrolls to Frank Clanton and his gang of highwaymen. "A
friend of mine told me about it, about how the robbers did
it,'' he added.

Clifton spread his hands helplessly. "I was told in every
case the damage from the blast and the wreck itself was so
extensive that no one could determine exactly how it was
done. We sent out one of our own line inspectors each time,
and he couldn't come up with anything conclusive. What

seems to be the most disturbing is how the robbers know which trains carry the money. Someone has to be giving the gang this information well in advance.''

''How far in advance does the army know when it plans to send a shipment?'' Slocum asked.

''Only a week, and they have varied their schedule twice to keep from using the same trains. Both times, the holdup men knew which train to derail.''

''It's hard to figure,'' Slocum agreed.

''I know Mr. Warren is highly agitated with me over the entire situation. Something had to be done. This is the reason why I contacted Mr. Huling down in Galveston. I've been authorized to offer him a substantial sum every time he rides with a payroll.''

''Sounds to me like you've done just about everything you can to safeguard the money.''

''I believe I have. I feel reasonably confident of our success this time. Mr. Huling has a frightful reputation when dealing with desperate men.''

''Seems like I've heard his name mentioned somewhere. Can't recall where or when.''

Clifton lowered his voice again. ''To tell the truth, I was told he's a professional killer. For the right amount of money he's said to be willing to kill someone outright, with no questions asked.''

''He sounds like a dangerous fellow,'' Slocum agreed, although he knew more about Huling than he'd admitted, even to Sheriff Dawson. Huling once did some work for the Pinkertons, and later the Union Pacific Railroad. In both cases he'd been fired for the use of violent methods when other means would have accomplished the same objectives. Huling was a remorseless sort with a fondness for shotguns and blood, the sort of thing neither the Pinkerton Agency nor the Union Pacific could tolerate when his penchant for killing made newspaper headlines in some of the wrong places.

''He *is* dangerous,'' Clifton confided. ''I was actually

afraid of him the day he came to this office to accept my proposition. He had this strange look in his eyes, like a man who isn't quite right in the head."

"Sometimes you have to fight fire with fire," Slocum said, to humor Clifton.

Clifton nodded. "Precisely. That is what I'm doing, with the full permission of the home office. These robberies have occurred far too often."

Slocum had all the information he needed from Clifton for the present, with once exception. He stood up and offered his hand. "Thanks for your time, Mr. Clifton. I may drop by later in the day to make sure the train to El Paso made it to Fort Stockton. I simply must know that the Texas and Pacific can provide me with a means of safe shipment for my valuable racehorses."

"I understand completely, Mr. Slocum," Clifton said, taking the hand Slocum extended, pumping it once. "Feel free to drop by anytime, and it was a genuine pleasure to make your acquaintance, although I'm still a bit puzzled as to why Mr. Warren thought I'd be interested in purchasing any of your horses."

"A simple mistake in understanding. It's not a problem, for as I said, I have a number of good customers in this area. Think nothing of it."

"Rest assured the Texas and Pacific will be able to ship your livestock without incident from now on, Mr. Slocum. I feel certain I have taken the proper measures."

Slocum nodded and turned to leave. "Let's hope for everyone's sake that Cletus Huling is as good as you believe he is. That will solve everything." He hesitated a moment. "By the way, are you acquainted with a woman by the name of Rose Miller? I'm told she's quite a beauty."

"Indeed I am," Clifton replied with obvious pride. "If you wish to meet her personally, I can arrange it."

"I don't think that'll be necessary," he told Clifton, with sweet recollections of last night's stay in her bed. "I have no plans to meet her, but I *was* told about her unusual beauty.''

"One of the most beautiful women in the world," Clifton said as Slocum headed for the door.

At least Willard Clifton was right when it came to his judgment of womanhood, Slocum thought.

7

Slocum walked back to the four-story St. Anthony Hotel, the best in San Antonio. He decided he'd saddle his horse at the livery behind it for a ride out to Fort Sam Houston on the north side of town. He had not lost his horse to a thief as he'd told Rose Miller, but an explanation for his arrival other than by train was needed, he felt, in order to convince her he wasn't working for the Texas and Pacific, looking into the train robberies for his old friend Malcom Warren. Slocum carried a letter from Malcom that he was to give to any military authorities he needed to question regarding the holdups. Based on what Willard Clifton told him, the trip out to the fort was probably a waste of time.

His deepest suspicions still lay with the railroad, with someone who worked for the company who knew the schedule for army payroll money. Clifton didn't seem like a dishonest man; however, he did know Rose Miller, and that alone could be enough to explain everything, if Clifton was telling Rose about the trains carrying army pay.

Based on his initial meeting with Clifton, it was more likely Clifton was giving out information without being aware that it was relayed to Frank Clanton and his gang. But until Slocum got to the bottom of things in San Antone, all was guesswork and supposition.

Before going to the stable, he ambled into the hotel dining room and took a table with a view of the river. The place was almost empty, because it was early, he supposed. After he ate, he intended to ride out to the fort, and by then, word should have come from Pandale or Fort Stockton as to the fate of the gold-laden Texas and Pacific train to El Paso.

A comely young waitress came over to his table. "What do you want for lunch, sir?" she asked, holding a stubby pencil above an order pad. "Our special today is chicken and dumplin's with boiled greens an' potatoes."

"Sounds perfect," he said, admiring her breasts underneath a stained white cotton blouse while she wrote down his order. "And a glass of brandy."

She was a dark brunette, with a lightly freckled face, and when he ordered brandy, her youthful innocence left her expression quickly. "You're an early drinker," she said, smiling at him. She had a full figure, oversized breasts, and a rounded butt poorly hidden under a calico skirt. "On my days off I like to go down to the river outside of town with a bottle of peach brandy. There's this swimmin' hole where hardly anybody goes an' after I've had a few sips of homemade brandy, I jump in the water to cool off. I reckon I shouldn't be tellin' this to a total stranger."

"Why not?" he asked. "I'd like to see this private swimming hole of yours sometime soon. Would you show it to me?"

"Wouldn't seem proper," she replied, blushing, averting her deep brown eyes.

"And why is that?"

"I don't even know your name."

"I'm John Slocum," he told her, grinning to lessen her discomfort as much as he could. "And I'd really like to see that swimming hole real soon. I'd buy a bottle of the best peach brandy in town and we could hire a carriage. I'd drive you out there . . . on your next day away from work."

"That's tomorrow," she said quietly, still unable to look at him.

"How about if I meet you at the livery stable behind this hotel tomorrow . . . let's say around noon, and we'll drive down the river. Nothing improper about that, Miss . . . ?"

"Claire. My name is Claire."

"You're a very pretty girl, Claire. I hope that wasn't an improper observation to make."

Her blush deepened. "Don't reckon it is, only it kinda embarrasses me. I know I ain't all that pretty, but it's nice of you to say so."

"You're quite pretty," he reassured her. "I don't mean to embarrass you, but it's true."

"You're a downright handsome man, Mr. Slocum. If you're sure you ain't funnin' me, I'll agree to go with that drive with you tomorrow. Only I ain't gonna swim."

"I'm not funning you at all, but why won't you go swimming with me?"

" 'Cause I ain't got no clothes on when I do, an' that sure enough wouldn't be proper at all."

He imagined what she would look like naked, swimming in a river, and despite the time he'd spent with Rose the previous evening, his cock began to stiffen inside his pants. "I would never ask a lady to do anything improper, Claire. I consider myself a gentleman and if you don't care to swim, perhaps you can sit on the riverbank and drink brandy while I enjoy the water."

"I suppose that'd be okay, only you'd have to wear some clothes . . . them short pants most men wear while they're swimmin' in a river."

"I'll do whatever you ask, Claire, so long as you agree to join me."

"I'll fetch you back your lunch, Mr. Slocum. I'll go with you tomorrow too."

"I wish you'd call me John."

Again, her face colored. "Maybe tomorrow I will. Be back with your chicken an' dumplin's in a minute."

He watched her hips sway beneath her skirt as she walked away toward the kitchen. He judged she was very young, perhaps eighteen or so. There were times when he craved a full-bodied woman like Claire. There was something about them. . . .

He cleaned his plate, and ate a bowl filled with plum cobbler that Claire brought. Then she gave him directions out to Fort Sam Houston, telling him which roads to take. Beyond the hotel window, as the dining room began to fill, buggies and more expensive carriages drove back and forth across San Antonio's streets.

He gave Claire a silver half-dollar for a tip as he was leaving the dining room, and when she held it in her hand her eyes rounded with surprise.

"How much change you want back from this?" she asked.

"None. It's for you. You gave me excellent service and I'm truly looking forward to our drive along the river tomorrow."

"But that's way too much!" she protested. "It's fifty cents an' your meal cost that much."

"Keep it," he said. "The service you gave me was better than the food."

He walked out while she was staring at his back, and he was certain that by tomorrow noon, Claire would be ready to drink brandy with him and swim without her clothes. Sometimes he got a feeling about women, and he had that feeling about Claire as he went upstairs to his spacious room, provided by Malcom Warren and the Texas and Pacific Railroad, to get his letter of introduction before he went around to the back of the St. Anthony to saddle his horse for the ride to the fort.

He'd been directed to the office of Colonel William Bush, in charge of U.S. Army disbursements to soldiers serving in the western sector of Texas, New Mexico Territory, and

Arizona Territory. After showing his letter of introduction to an orderly at a front desk, Slocum was admitted into the colonel's office.

Colonel Bush was a wiry man with gray sideburns and deep wrinkles on his sun-darkened face. He shook hands with Slocum and pointed to a chair while a squad of infantrymen paraded across the fort compound beyond his window.

"Mr. Warren advised me someone might be coming to investigate the robberies," Bush said. "A private detective, I think he said."

"I'm no private detective," Slocum replied. "I've worked for some of the railroads a few times, but this isn't my profession. Malcom Warren is an old friend. When his own people at the Texas and Pacific couldn't come up with anything on Frank Clanton or these holdups, he wired me and asked me if I'd come down to nose around a bit."

"Washington will force us to use other means of shipment for our payrolls," Bush said, "if this continues."

"Understandable. The army has lost a lot of money in this affair."

Bush nodded. "We'll have to find other means of getting our payrolls to remote posts in West Texas and the territories. The men must be paid, and there are no banks close enough to places like Fort Grant in Arizona Territory. Sending an armed escort with a wagon is time-consuming and expensive."

"And just as risky, unless the escort is large enough to discourage Clanton."

"I quite agree, Mr. Slocum. Have you any ideas how this can be happening?"

"I've talked to Willard Clifton at the Texas and Pacific office. He says the information for Clanton isn't coming from any of his people."

"We're equally certain it isn't coming from my office. But somehow Clanton knows which trains carry the most money well in advance. That must mean he as a source of information here at Fort Sam, or with the Texas and Pacific. There is no other rational conclusion anyone can draw from events.''

''I'd agree.''

''As you may know,'' the colonel continued, ''we have a payroll shipment that is overdue at Fort Stockton this very morning. We haven't heard whether the train arrived. Mr. Clifton has assured me he'll let me know the minute it does.''

''Do you know about the shootist Clifton hired to guard the money along with your escort?''

''Yes, I do. A man with a dark past, I'm afraid. Allan Pinkerton fired him years ago, and his record is very poor with other rail companies. I'd call him a bounty hunter rather than any sort of shootist.''

''I know Cletus Huling . . . by reputation.''

''Then you may also know the railroad has posted a one-thousand-dollar reward for Clanton's capture. I suspect this is the reason Mr. Huling is aboard that train . . . he wants a chance to kill Clanton for the reward money. The salary he's being paid is probably not nearly as important to him.''

''I hadn't heard about the thousand-dollar reward,'' Slocum said, thinking it odd that Malcom had never mentioned it in any of his telegrams or letters.

''Like something dead, that much money draws flies. And buzzards like Huling.''

''It's just past noon. Clifton should have word by now if his train made it.''

''He'll send someone out to inform me either way. I know he's as worried as we are . . . unless, on the off chance, he has something to do with the holdups, which seems highly unlikely in my estimation.''

''I don't have him figured for a crook either,'' Slocum told the colonel. ''But there may be another possibility. A woman by the name of Rose Miller keeps company with Clifton at times, or so I was told by Sheriff Dawson. Clifton, in the heat of passion, may be telling her things he shouldn't.''

"Every man in San Antonio knows who Rose Miller is. She is a remarkable beauty.''

"I . . . met her last night. Briefly.''

"And you suspect she may have some connection to Frank Clanton?''

"Can't prove it yet. I may be wrong.''

Bush stared at him with rheumy eyes. "I am only sure of one thing at this point, that the information isn't coming from any of my men.''

"You've done enough checking?''

"A very thorough job. No one who knows about the payroll shipments has been overlooked. Perhaps it has all ended now, I dare to hope. Word that Cletus Huling was aboard this particular train may have reached the Clanton gang.''

"I've heard of Clanton before. He's kin to the James boys up in Missouri, I was told. . . .'' As Slocum spoke they heard a horse gallop up to the front of the colonel's office. The outer door burst open and a thin voice shouted, "Tell Colonel Bush the train to El Paso has been robbed again! I just came from the Texas an' Pacific office.''

Bush stiffened in his seat. Slocum got up from his chair to walk to the door.

"I'm with the main office of the Texas and Pacific,'' he said to a slender boy who was obviously out of breath after making a fast ride out to the fort. "How did it happen? Did Mr. Clifton tell you?''

"It got knocked off the tracks, was all he said, an' that six soldiers was dead. Four passengers was killed, an' some gunfighter by the name of Huling was dead too.''

"Cletus Huling was killed?'' Colonel Bush asked as he came to the outer office to stand beside Slocum.

"That's what Mr. Clifton tol' me to tell you . . . six soldiers is dead, an' four passengers. Two men who run the train was burnt alive when the engine exploded. Then he said to tell you this feller named Huling got killed.''

Colonel Bush turned to Slocum. ''Apparently I was wrong in my first judgment regarding Cletus Huling. He wasn't enough of a shootist to escape this robbery with his life.''

8

The big bay thoroughbred stud galloped easily from the hills north of San Antonio where Fort Sam Houston lay to the center of town and the railroad depot. Slocum pulled his horse to a halt at the Texas and Pacific Railroad Company office and swung down. He needed all the information Willard Clifton had before he set out to see where the robbery had occurred and to scout for tracks.

Clifton's young clerk was ashed-faced when Slocum walked in, and he merely pointed to Clifton's office. Slocum came into the office unannounced.

Clifton had a bottle of whiskey on his desk. He barely glanced up upon Slocum's arrival.

"I guess you heard the news," Clifton said.

"I did. I was at Colonel Bush's office when the messenger boy showed up."

"They *knew*!" Clifton snapped, tossing back a smudged shot glass of whiskey.

"That's mighty obvious. Now we've gotta find out *how* they knew about the payroll."

"I'm finished with this company," Clifton said, sighing heavily. "I'll be fired immediately, as soon as word reaches the home office. I've already sent the telegram." Clifton seemed to be genuinely concerned, not a man who secretly stood to profit from the robbery.

"Tell me how it happened. As much as you know," Slocum said. "Give me all the details."

Clifton wiped his brow with a soggy handkerchief and poured himself another drink. "The wire from Fort Stockton reported it occurred about fifteen miles into the canyon."

"And?"

"All it said was the locomotive crew was dead, six soldiers were shot down, and four passengers are dead. Many more passengers are seriously injured. This is the end of my career with the Texas and Pacific."

"The payroll is gone, I take it."

"The safe was blown open with dynamite. That's about all I know. A doctor from Fort Stockton is driving down in a buggy to care for the injured passengers. According to the wire from our water stop at Pandale, the train is a total wreck and the baggage car was blown to bits."

Slocum watched a troop of mounted cavalry trotting their horses down the tracks, headed westward. "Colonel Bush is sending out a patrol to look for evidence, any tracks the gang might have left behind," he said.

"It's too late for me," Clifton whimpered, tossing back half of his drink. "As I told you, I wired the Fort Worth office. They'll be sending me my notice any minute now, and I'm sure my replacement will be boarding the next train from Fort Worth to San Antonio."

"I intend to ride out to the scene of the robbery myself, to look it over," Slocum said. "Just one more thing I need to know. Did you speak to anyone about this train and its payload beforehand?"

Clifton looked up from his desk as though the question surprised him. "Of course not."

"Since you learned the date of the payroll's departure, have you seen the woman Rose Miller?"

He looked askance at Slocum. "A week ago, possibly.

We had dinner and a few drinks, that's all."

"But did you know about the shipment then?"

"Why do you ask, Mr. Slocum? Rose wouldn't have anything to do with an outlaw like Frank Clanton. Are you implying that Rose might have something to do with these robberies?"

"I'm looking at every possibility. I don't think she's actually involved. I was only curious. I have to start somewhere."

"But not with Rose. Surely not. She's a decent woman with no ties to men like Clanton. I'm sure of it."

Slocum turned away from the desk. "I'm going to ask Sheriff Dawson to send one of his deputies out with me to Devil's River Canyon. I may be gone for a few days."

Clifton seemed puzzled. "What's your real interest in this, Mr. Slocum? You said you were in the horse business."

"I am. However, Malcom is my friend. The messenger said you were told Cletus Huling was killed in the robbery."

"That's what the telegram from Fort Stockton said. Huling was found shot to death, along with the military men. Huling was listed as one of the passengers."

"I'm riding over to the sheriff's office to talk to him. As late as it is, I'll probably wait until morning to ride out, and I have a few other things I want to look into in the meantime. I was informed it's a hard three-day ride on horseback to the canyon. I'm sure the robbers have crossed over into Mexico by now. I'm curious to see if I can find where they cross the river."

Clifton took more whiskey. "I can save you some time, as long as I'm still in charge of the San Antonio office of this company. Tomorrow I'm sending out a repair crew with several flatcars loaded with equipment and new track. You'll be there far sooner if you ride the rails to the holdup scene."

It sounded like an easier trip, although he'd be missing

his appointment to go swimming with Claire. "I may take you up on that offer. After I talk to Sheriff Dawson, I'll let you know one way or the other. If you can couple a cattle car to this same engine, I'll have a horse to look for tracks when we get there."

"Easily done. Easily done," Clifton replied, his shoulders rounded. "Let me know if you need the cattle car for your horse and I can have it added to the train. Because of the damage to the tracks and the derailed cars and locomotive, the line must be cleared . . . that is, if I'm still with the company. I'm assembling our eight-man repair crew now and ordering coffins for the dead. A train from El Paso is backing slowly toward the crash scene to carry the rest of our passengers to their destinations. It will take the rest of today and all night to assemble a repair crew and load the flatcars. The train should pull out sometime in the morning, if all goes well."

"I'll let you know about the cattle car," Slocum said. "One more thing I forgot to ask, and I suppose I should have asked Colonel Bush. Where is the payroll kept until it's put on the train?"

"At the Planters Bank over on Presa Street," Clifton answered, appearing to be puzzled by the question. "A mounted army squad comes with a wagon to escort it to the train and see that it's safely loaded. Then, an unspecified number of foot soldiers board the baggage car to stand guard over the vault."

"I wonder if anyone at the bank knows ahead of time when the money is to be shipped. That's another thing I intended to ask the colonel . . . we were interrupted in the midst of our discussion when your messenger arrived." Slocum had stumbled upon a connection he hadn't counted on. The president of the Planters Bank was also Rose Miller's silent partner in the Velvet Slipper. It was too much to be sheer coincidence.

"I would assume they notify the president of the bank, Mr. Herring, sometime in advance," Clifton said. "Although I don't know all of the army's procedures in these matters, I understand the money comes from Washington by train. It reaches San Antonio from our office in Fort Worth. The times of shipment are a closely guarded secret, as I'm sure you must have guessed by now. No payroll trains between San Antonio and Fort Worth have ever been robbed. But when our train leaves for the west, it crosses some of the most forbidding country anyone can imagine. Unsettled cattle and goat country, for the most part. And this is where our problems have developed. Clanton can ride up from Mexico virtually undetected, it would seem, to waylay our trains in Devil's River Canyon and ride back across the border. There simply isn't any way to guard every mile of track between here and El Paso. We have armed inspectors who examine the tracks in handcars on a weekly basis to make certain all sections are joined properly. Two of our employees stationed at the Pandale water stop travel through Devil's River Canyon once a week to inspect the rails. Since there is no telegraph in Pandale, they must make the inspections on Wednesday mornings when no trains are scheduled. They rarely ever report seeing any-one near the canyon. It's one of the driest regions you can imagine. Scarcely good enough for grazing any livestock.''

Slocum nodded. ''I've ridden through some of that part of Texas. The place where these robberies are happening is remote . . . empty as hell. But Clanton has to know which trains to rob in order to be so successful every time he pulls a job. That information has to come from someone in the army, at the bank where the money's kept, or from this railroad.''

Clifton closed his eyelids a moment. ''How well I know,'' he said softly. ''Everyone at the home office is pointing a finger straight at me. Mr. Warren has been very understanding, until now. This will be the last straw, I fear.''

One burning question needed to be asked. ''Just how far

in advance do you know about the payroll shipments?'' said Slocum.

"In most cases it's about a week. I have to make sure we have a baggage car with a large safe available. Colonel Bush notifies me.''

"Does he notify you personally?''

"No,'' Clifton replied. "He sends a Sergeant Baker. The colonel assures me Baker is honest, a career military man with a spotless record.''

"I'm sure Colonel Bush has investigated Baker and anyone else who knows about the shipments in advance,'' Slocum said. "I reckon that leaves the possibility that someone at the bank can be a source Clanton uses. I'll make a few inquiries at the bank on Malcom's behalf. I'll let you know this afternoon if I need that cattle car.''

"It won't be a problem,'' Clifton said as Slocum nodded and walked out of the office.

Outside, he glanced up and down the depot platform and the loading docks. Clifton had revealed what could turn out to be another important bit of information. If the same soldier, Sergeant Baker, rode to the Texas and Pacific office to advise of a money shipment, the answer to all the robberies could be as simple as someone putting two and two together. An observer standing near the office who saw Sergeant Baker go inside might be able to conclude that arrangements, always a week in advance, were being made for a baggage car with a large iron vault. The observer could then send word to Clanton. Was the solution this simple? he wondered. Still, the tie-in between the bank and Rose bothered him. Even if Clifton were totally innocent of wrongdoing, he could be telling Rose things without realizing what their implications might be.

Mounting his stallion, Slocum decided it was doubtful that the news was sent to Clanton by an observer. It would depend on how many trains pulled out for El Paso exactly a week after Sergeant Baker requested a baggage car with a safe. Clanton's information had never been wrong, according to Malcom and Willard Clifton. Five times now, Clanton had robbed only the correct trains passing through Devil's River Canyon, and nobody could be that lucky in five instances, never guessing wrong.

Slocum reined toward the center of town to find Sheriff Dawson and talk to Mr. Herring at the Planters Bank. Ike Dawson was a native of South Texas and he would know where to look for the closest border crossing below Devil's River Canyon. Slocum made up his mind to help Malcom Warren, to find out not only who was giving information to Frank Clanton, but also where Clanton was hiding in Mexico. With some luck he might track down Clanton, and if the opportunity came, take back this last stolen payroll, or what was left of it after the robbers celebrated their latest success. Unlike duly authorized peace officers in Texas, Slocum could cross the international boundary freely, and if he chose to act against Clanton, it would be as a private citizen.

Riding back into town, Slocum remembered he knew a *comandante* of the *federales* in Villa Acuna, across the river from Del Rio. Porfirio Valdez was a powerful man in northern Mexico even at a time when revolution threatened south of the border. If Slocum went after Clanton in Mexico, he'd have an ally if Valdez was still in command of the garrison in Villa Acuna.

For now, about all he could do was try to find the source of the information regarding the payrolls, and if that led him to Mexico, Slocum could consider his options then.

He found the sheriff's office across from the stone court house not far from the ruins of the Alamo, where brave Texans had made a valiant stand many years before against an overwhelming force of Mexican soldiers under General Santa Anna. While the old Alamo chapel was crumbling now, it was something of a shrine to loyal Texans, who remembered the lives lost there.

He tied off his horse in front of the sheriff's office and

strode in, and was greeted by a bearded deputy with a scowl on his face.

"I need to see Sheriff Dawson," Slocum said.

"He's out at Fort Sam," the deputy replied, rocking back in his chair behind a battered wooden desk. "In case you ain't heard yet, there's been another train got robbed out west of here an' Ike's gone to find out about it."

"I've heard. I just left the office of the Texas and Pacific, talking to Mr. Clifton about it."

"What's your interest in the robbery?" the deputy asked suspiciously with a flickering glance at Slocum's cross-draw holster and gun.

"I work for the railroad," Slocum replied. "They sent me down to investigate what's going on."

The deputy gave him a mirthless chuckle. "Hope you do some better'n the last gun they hired. Them outlaws killed him, Ike said, an' he was supposed to be a bad hombre."

Slocum backed away to the door. "I may be a little harder to kill," he said. "Tell Sheriff Dawson that John Slocum came by to talk to him. I'll come back later this afternoon."

9

The Planters Bank sat opposite the town square, a white rock building with windows looking out on the courthouse lawns. When Slocum walked in, he noticed an armed guard cradling a shotgun not far from the tellers' cages. San Antonio was still a rough town at times, close enough to the Mexican border to have its share of dangerous visitors passing through on their way to hide from the law below the Rio Grande.

To the left of the bank lobby, an elderly woman with silver hair in a twisted bun sat at a desk in front of an office marked "Private." Slocum strolled over to the desk to speak to the woman.

"I'd like to see a Mr. Sheldon Herring," he told her. "I'm with the Texas and Pacific Railroad Company. It's regarding the army payroll shipments deposited here. My name is John Slocum and I have a letter of introduction from the railroad's vice president, Mr. Malcom Warren."

Her glance fell to the gun he was carrying. "I'll speak with Mr. Herring. Please wait a moment."

She got up and entered the private office, after a soft knock. She closed the door behind her while Slocum watched the busy street in front of the bank ... horsemen and buggies and carriages and heavy freight wagons passing in both directions. The city was a beehive of activity on this particular spring day. Waiting, he decided he needed to investigate the telegraph office there, to see if one of the operators remembered the same person sending a wire to a town along the Mexican border a week before each of the holdups. Someone should know. He also wondered if it could be Rose.

"Mr. Herring will see you now," the woman said as she came out of the office, holding the door open for him.

"Thank you, ma'am," he told her, tipping his Stetson as he removed it to enter the office.

A hawk-nosed man in a dark blue business suit got up from behind a polished oak desk. He regarded Slocum with a look that could have been suspicion.

Slocum removed the letter from Malcom Warren from his coat pocket and handed it across the desk. "I'm John Slocum," he said as he left his hand out for a shake.

"Sheldon Herring," the banker said, after he took the letter and shook hands. He unfolded the letter and read it quickly as he was sitting back down. "It says here that you are a special investigator for the Texas and Pacific. I assume it has to do with the recent robberies. Please have a seat."

Herring gave no evidence he knew about the latest holdup. "It would seem I got here too late," Slocum said, sitting in one of two chairs across the desk.

"And how is that, Mr. Slocum? Surely you came here to see what you could find out. Why do you feel you got here too late to be of service to the railroad?"

"Another train was robbed last night. That makes five in less than a year."

Herring's complexion paled somewhat. "Dear God," he said in a whisper, handing the letter back to Slocum. "Mr. Clifton told me he'd hired a security guard to assist the soldiers, a man by the name of Huling, I believe. From Galveston, I think he said. He was supposed to be very good at this sort of thing."

"Cletus Huling. He was shot to death during the robbery.

I was told the train was derailed. Six soldiers were killed, as well as four passengers and two trainmen.''

Herring swallowed. ''This has become almost absurd. Did the robbery occur in Devil's River Canyon?''

''Same place. And always a train carrying a big army payroll to West Texas. Somebody has inside information. It's all too obvious.''

''Have you spoken with Colonel Bush at Fort Sam Houston?''

''Just now. I was at the fort when he found out about the robbery. He's convinced no one at the fort is involved, which only leaves someone working for the railroad here, or someone who knows when the money is going to leave your bank vaults.''

Herring appeared to be listening to the sounds of wagons outside his office window a moment. ''Two Texas Rangers came the last time this happened. They asked who at this bank knew when the shipments were leaving. I told them I was the only one who was informed ahead of time, which is true. It's almost as if I am suspected by the Texas Rangers of being involved somehow in the robberies.''

''Somebody *has* to be giving these outlaws the information or they'd make a mistake and rob the wrong trains. But they don't, and that is pretty solid proof that they know the schedules for each shipment,'' Slocum said, reading Herring's face for any sign that he might be hiding something.

''That, unfortunately for someone, is abundantly clear,'' Herring said. ''I do understand being questioned about it, yet I have a position of high responsibility here. If I wanted to rob the United States Army, all I'd have to do is open the vault on any given night and leave for another country . . . South America, or someplace where I could never be found.'' He gave Slocum a steely stare. ''Who and where do you think the information is coming from, Mr. Slocum? I trust you have an opinion.''

''Not yet. I'm still looking around.''

"I'll cooperate in any way you wish, of course. I wouldn't want the bank to get a bad reputation."

"Mr. Clifton and Mr. Warren with the railroad have the same concerns. I'm sure you understand. I have spoken with Sheriff Ike Dawson. A man by the name of Frank Clanton is being credited with the robberies and he's apparently very clever. He knows which trains carry the army money. He is clearly getting this information from someone in San Antonio. My job is to find out who that is."

"I'm the only suspect you can have at this bank," Herring said. "I can't speak for the railroad company or the army, but if you're a thorough man you'll check at both places. Colonel Bush makes the decisions for the army as to when the money is to be sent. Mr. Clifton is advised at the same time, I believe, in order to secure the right type of railroad car. A soldier under Colonel Bush then informs me, so I can have the funds ready for shipment in canvas bags. A week later, on the specified date, a unit of soldiers comes to the bank with an authorization signed by Colonel Bush for withdrawal, a writ to obtain the amount of money he requires. This has been our standard procedure for a number of years. Government regulations require it."

"Is it the same soldier who informs you every time?" Slocum asked.

"Indeed it is, a sergeant by the name of Baker."

Another possible connection, Slocum thought. Baker was a common figure in the process each time. While it was certain Colonel Bush had questioned Baker, Slocum made a mental note to ask Baker a few questions himself. Perhaps it was someone Baker knew that he told about the shipments. It was worth checking into.

"And this system for taking the money out, putting it on the train, is always the same?" Slocum continued.

"It has never varied, not that I recall."

"It's the same person then."

"Probably. I can't believe it has happened again. Not with all the precautions the railroad took."

"By that you mean Cletus Huling."

"Yes, and several additional soldiers, according to Colonel Bush when I spoke with him last week."

"This same Sergeant Baker came to inform you of the date, and it was precisely one week from the day Baker told you about it?"

"That is correct. It would seem that Sergeant Baker and I are prime suspects. I assure you it's circumstantial in my case. I have very large responsibilities."

"I'm sure you do, Mr. Herring. The Texas and Pacific may be forced to change its depository and the rail line contract, unless I can come up with some answers."

"Naturally. The government can't afford to keep losing so much money. What I can't understand is how this gang eludes all efforts at capture."

Slocum noticed a slight shaking in Herring's fingertips. "I feel sure they hide out down in Mexico after they pull a job. It just makes sense."

"Someone in San Antonio must be sharing in the profits from their enterprise," Herring observed.

Slocum decided to take a chance, in order to judge Herring's reaction. "On the subject of sharing profits, I understand you own part of the Velvet Slipper."

The banker's pupils became pinpoints. "What does that have to do with your investigation, Mr. Slocum?"

"Probably nothing."

"Then why did you ask?"

He would only reveal part of the truth for now. "I learned that both you and Willard Clifton know Rose Miller. It may be only a coincidence."

"My ownership in the Velvet Slipper has nothing to do with the robberies or the Texas and Pacific rail line," Herring said, and he was emphatic about it. "Rose is simply a business partner and nothing else. I was unaware that Mr. Clifton was acquainted with her."

Slocum stood up. "I'm turning over every rock, Mr. Herring, in order to find out who's informing Frank Clanton and his gang. It's no crime to own an interest in a saloon. I'll be talking to Sheriff Dawson and the Texas Rangers. There are some questions I must ask.''

Herring got out of his chair. ''As I told you before, I am more than happy to cooperate.'' He shook hands with Slocum and showed him to the door.

Slocum left the bank with the distinct impression that he'd struck a nerve by mentioning Rose Miller to the banker. But the connection didn't fit yet . . . he'd have to keep working on it until there was something solid. Or nothing at all.

Sheriff Dawson was still away from his office when Slocum looked in. The same surly deputy offered little in the way of information, unless he was asked.

''Where is the Texas Rangers' office?''

''Across the river. Ain't far from the old Alamo, if you know where that's at.''

Slocum let himself out of the office with his mind made up to inform Clifton he would need the cattle car for his horse. It was getting more difficult to get what he wanted by asking for information here.

Many times, Slocum found what he was looking for by simply looking for the physical evidence.

''I'll be taking my horse,'' he told Clifton, noting that the bottle on the man's desk was half empty. ''Have you heard from the Fort Worth office or from Malcom?''

''Not a word,'' Clifton said hoarsely. ''That's what has me worried. My replacement is surely on the way to San Antonio as we speak.''

Slocum meant to ignore that for the moment. ''What time does the train leave for Devil's River Canyon in the morning?''

''No later than eight. Men are loading the flatcars now with new rails and cross-ties and spikes. It's a difficult job to clear damaged tracks when there's been a derailment like this. I need time to make sure everything is aboard before the train pulls out.''

''I'll be here at seven with my horse and gear,'' Slocum told him. ''I want good hay and oats in the cattle car for my stallion. I only give him the best of care.''

''I'll make sure of it myself,'' Clifton said. ''If I'm still with the Texas and Pacific Railroad Company tomorrow morning.''

Slocum made to leave. ''I doubt if Malcom will do anything until he hears from me.''

''Did you find out anything from Sheriff Dawson?''

''Not yet. He wasn't in his office. Mr. Herring at the bank told me the Texas Rangers have investigated some of the previous robberies.''

''So they have. Captain Ford is the man you want to talk to, only the Rangers couldn't come up with anything the last time it happened.''

''I'll ask for Captain Ford. See you in the morning, Mr. Clifton . . . and if I was you, I'd leave that bottle alone for a spell.''

''It's the only thing that calms my nerves. I don't know where I'll find another job.''

''The best thing to do now is help the home office do whatever it can to clear the tracks and see to the injured passengers. You didn't ask me for advice, but I'm giving it to you anyway.''

''Of course you're right,'' Clifton said. ''I suppose I'm only feeling sorry for myself.''

Slocum left the office to find the Texas Rangers. And he was thinking about Claire . . . how he'd miss that swimming trip at the river tomorrow.

On a hunch, he'd pay her a call at the hotel dining room tonight, if for no better reason than to explain and offer his apology.

10

He sat at a corner table sipping brandy and smoking a cigar. It was almost ten o'clock and the dining room was closing. He'd eaten a good steak and spoken to Claire about the necessity of leaving town tomorrow morning, with an apology. To his surprise, she had offered to show him her swimming spot tonight as soon as she got off work. He'd told her he'd rent a carriage, but she'd said it wasn't far and they could walk beside the river. A pleasant evening loomed before Slocum at the end of a very long day of frustration.

Texas Ranger Captain Bob Ford had pulled out for the site of the train wreck only hours before Slocum reached the Ranger office, another stroke of bad luck. An army patrol and two Rangers were headed for the scene, and Slocum hoped the work train would get him there ahead of everyone else, before any hoofprints could be disturbed.

He'd talked to Sheriff Dawson right after sundown. Dawson had nothing new to add to what Slocum already knew . . . with one possible exception. A local saloon drunk by the name of Collins who often gave the sheriff scraps of information regarding crimes in the city had told Dawson that he'd nearly swear, for the price of a drink, that he'd seen Frank Clanton in San Antonio about a year ago, before the robberies started. And for the price of another drink he'd related *where* he'd spotted Clanton—on a late-night visit to the Velvet Slipper through a back door.

When Slocum first heard this bit of news he'd been convinced he was onto something, until the sheriff had admitted that Billy Collins wasn't always reliable, that sometimes he'd say anything for a drink. "I wouldn't put too much stock in it," Dawson had said, "but it tends to add to them rumors I told you about when you got to town. Maybe ol' Collins heard it somewhere. Or maybe he did see Clanton that night. No way to tell for sure if Collins is tellin' the truth or just repeatin' somethin' he overheard in a back alley."

It mattered little right now, Slocum decided, although it could be an important piece in the puzzle. Tracking Clanton to Mexico was more important . . . if it could be done. The sheriff had said a gang of outlaws could cross the Rio Grande most anyplace this year, because the river was low and it had been a dry year upriver, keeping it that way. "My guess would be Piedras Negras where the *federales* don't look real close at things," he'd said, when asked to speculate on where Clanton might be hiding out below the border.

Claire came toward his table as glass lamps were being put out around the dining room. She smiled and said, "Almost ready, Mr. Slocum. I put the bottle of peach brandy you paid for in a paper bag. It's with my shawl. I should be ready to go in a few minutes."

"It's a nice night outside," he told her. "Cool, not like Texas in the summer."

"It does get awfully hot here," she agreed as she headed to the kitchen. Slocum wondered if Claire also got awfully hot when the right man applied liquor and romance to an evening spent with her. He'd glimpsed the laces on a corset when the front of her blouse had opened between buttons. He tried to imagine what it would be like opening the laces girding her magnificent breasts. And her naked hips would be just as pleasant to look at, if she gave him the chance. She was young, but not so young that she didn't know about the taste of peach brandy. Claire might be more experienced than he'd thought when he'd first set eyes on her at lunchtime. She had been more than willing to go for a walk beside the river tonight, hardly the sort of thing an innocent young girl would do with a man she'd just met today. Prospects seemed good for an opportunity to know her intimately.

Ten minutes later, she came out of the kitchen wearing her shawl around her shoulders, carrying a bag with the brandy. "I'm ready," she said as he stood by the door. "Carlos and Belle will lock up after we leave."

He took her by the arm and escorted her away from the dining room at the St. Anthony Hotel, strolling toward the river. The streets were all but empty in this section of town after ten, and they encountered only a few pedestrians and an occasional buggy on their way to the riverbank.

Claire was beaming when he glanced at her. She had her hand in the crook of his arm. "Turn this way," she said. "There's a path going under those two bridges. Won't be nobody else out this late, so we'll have the river all to ourselves once we get past the edge of town."

"I'm glad you were willing to show me your swimming hole tonight," he said. "I sure hate the fact that I'm having to leave on business in the morning."

"You said it had something to do with the railroad. Is it that robbery? Nearly everybody who came in was talkin' about how it happened, that folks was killed an' all the money on the train got stole."

"Every now and then I do a little work for some of the rail lines. Let's not talk about work. Why don't you tell me a little bit about yourself . . . where you grew up and what you like to do with your spare time."

She giggled. "I like to go swimmin' an' drink peach brandy in the summer, like I already told you. It's nearly warm enough now to go swimmin' . . ."

* * *

Claire held the bottle to her lips, taking a healthy swallow before she gave it to him. They sat beneath a drooping willow tree listening to the soft gurgling sounds made by the river as it flowed past. Scattered lights from the city were almost half a mile away. Lightning bugs winked at them from trees along the water's edge. Somewhere close by, a bullfrog croaked. The sky was alive with twinkling stars.

He'd taken off his split-tail coat and placed it on the ground behind her, curling his gunbelt near his feet where his Stetson lay in the grass. "This sure is a nice quiet place," he said.

"The river's deep enough here to swim," she said, "even if this is a real dry year."

Hearing her say how dry it was reminded him of the remark made by Sheriff Dawson about the Rio Grande. But the girl beside him would keep him from thinking much about Frank Clanton and the stolen money. That could wait until tomorrow. "It looks so damn inviting I may have to take a swim right now," he said, "after I have a bit more brandy. But you'd have to promise to turn the other way while I took my clothes off. Of course, you'd do that anyway, being a proper young lady like you are, I'm sure."

She spoke as he was downing more brandy. "I wouldn't look till you said it was okay," she promised, "after you got in the water so I couldn't see you naked an' all."

"That would be perfect," he said, giving her the bottle. "I just know that water's gonna feel mighty good."

"I'm right sure it will," she replied, "even if it is a bit chilly tonight. I don't suppose it's all that cold." Claire let her shawl fall off her shoulders as she took another drink and licked her lips.

He decided there was no point in waiting any longer, for the girl had already consumed a goodly amount of liquor. "Turn your head the other way so I can undress. I'll keep my back to you so nothing will show."

From the corner of his eye he saw her smile briefly as he stood up to take off his shirt. "I won't peek," she said while he was unbuttoning his shirtfront.

He pulled off his boots and socks and then shucked down his pants, his back turned to her. Standing naked on a soft carpet of grass, he said, "I'm going in. However, I sure could use one more sip of that brandy, in case the water's really cold."

She handed him the bottle slowly. He was forced to turn to her to reach it, and when he did he found her staring at his limp cock dangling between his legs.

"Oh, my goodness!" she exclaimed, without looking away.

"What's wrong?" he asked, taking the brandy as if nothing was wrong with being naked in front of her.

"You have . . . the biggest . . . thing I've ever seen," she stammered. "I know I shouldn't be looking . . . ."

"It's okay with me if you look." He drank deeply, knowing what lay in store for him now.

"How do you ever . . . fit it inside . . . a woman?" she asked in a tiny, timid voice, continuing to stare at his cock.

"It fits. Women seem to like it."

"But what happens . . . ? I know I shouldn't be saying this, but what happens when . . . it gets hard? Doesn't it get even bigger then?"

"Some. If you wouldn't think it was the improper thing to do, I'd gladly show you."

"Oh, Mr. Slocum! That would be *very* improper, although I would dearly love to know . . . how big it gets. I suppose you'll think I'm naughty for saying it."

"Not at all. In fact, I think it's quite nice that you can be so frank about wanting to see it get larger. That would not be the least bit improper as far as I'm concerned."

"Dearie me! I feel so warm all of a sudden. It must be the brandy."

He stepped closer to where she sat, so that his cock was a few inches from her face, a cock that was beginning to swell. "I will need your hand for a moment."

"My hand?"

"Yes, but only for a moment. Let me show you." He bent over and took her right hand, then placed her palm gently around the base of his prick. "There," he went on, enjoying the look of rapture in her eyes as she stared at his member so near her lovely face. "Now move your hand back and forth like this." He jacked her dainty hand up and down by holding her wrist.

Claire's fingers curled around his stiffening cock as it came erect. She did not show the slightest reluctance to hold or pump his prick. "It's . . . the biggest one I've ever seen," she whispered, tracing the tip of her tongue across her lips after she said it.

"A few women have told me it really feels good inside them," he said.

"I'm quite sure it does," she remarked, pumping harder, faster, until his prick stuck out from his body. "If a woman could make it fit. I know I must seem dreadfully naughty to be doing this to you."

"I like it," he said hoarsely.

With a suddenness that surprised him, she plunged the head of his cock into her mouth, coming to her knees, flicking the end of her tongue over his prick.

"That really feels good," he said with a sigh.

She made soft sucking sounds, and began to bob her head back and forth, taking him deeper into her mouth, her warm lips closed gently around his shaft. Seconds later she began unbuttoning her blouse hurriedly, a low moaning coming from her throat, yet she kept on sucking and moving her head.

Her blouse flew off and she went quickly to her corset strings, still sucking his cock, unfastening the laces. Creamy mounds of quivering flesh spilled over the top of her undergarment until at last, two huge breasts sprang free. Slocum stared down at them in utter fascination, rosy nipples twisted hard, a sight any man longed to see.

Claire stopped sucking just as suddenly as she'd begun, and looked up at him. "Put it inside me," she said. "I just know it's gonna feel real good."

She unfastened her skirt and wriggled out of it and her corset while lying on her back in the grass. She had smooth, rounded thighs. In the light from the stars he could see her huge breasts, like twin snowy-white mountains in the Rockies.

He knelt between her thighs and lay over her as gently as he could, guiding his throbbing cock into the soft hair around the lips of her cunt. She was wet when his prick touched her, as if her juices flowed like the river beside them.

Slocum entered her, finding her cunt as warm and wet as her mouth, but he soon felt resistance when only the head of his cock was forced into her opening.

"Oh, Mr Slocum!" she gasped, rocking, clamping her legs over his buttocks.

He clasped one pillow-soft breast in his left hand, finding it too large to cover with his palm and fingers. When he squeezed it, her thrusting against his shaft increased.

"More," she said. "I want more!"

He granted her request, shoving his prick all the way to the hilt with one mighty push. Claire sucked in a breath of air and started to hammer her cunt into his groin with faster and faster movements.

Slocum returned her thrusts with his own, adding power by curling his toes into the grass. The girl made whimpering noises, and she grabbed two fistfuls of his hair. The tempo of their lovemaking increased.

His testicles contracted, rising, and he could feel his jism rushing into his shaft at the same moment as Claire let out a stifled scream, her lips pressed together in a feeble attempt to contain her cry. She rose off the ground despite his weight and went rigid, straining, reaching for her climax with every muscle in her body.

His seed exploded from his balls, flooding her womb,

and the ecstasy of it made him forget about wrecked trains and stolen payrolls and everything else.

Later, he lay in her arms totally spent, waiting for his rapid heartbeat to slow.

11

Frank Clanton's wounds from the shotgun pellets were far worse than he'd thought, and now his left arm showed angry streaks of red around some of the tiny holes. Pus leaked out of several tears in his skin where his shirt had been shredded by Cletus Huling's final shotgun blast.

"Looks like them's gonna get worse," Raymond Polk said as they trotted their horses to the banks of the Rio Grande above Villa Acuna.

"I'll need a doctor," Frank agreed, dabbing at some of the worst swollen spots where lead was embedded in his skin. "We'll stop for tequila an' some food in Acuna tonight. Can't stay long on account of that bastard Valdez."

"Who'd have ever thought there'd be an honest Meskin in the *federales*?" Bob Walls observed while he searched both quiet riverbanks for signs of life.

Frank stopped tending to his arm and shoulder long enough to examine the river himself. "Looks okay to cross. Oughta be dark soon."

"Maybe we oughta wait till dark," Raymond suggested.

"Like hell!" Frank snapped. "There'll be Texas Rangers or a posse comin' right behind us, if they pick up our tracks. This money ain't ours till we cross over, 'less we aim to fight 'em for it again."

"Sure is a passel of money," Lefty said, squinting across at the Mexican side of the river in the last rays of sun coming from the west. "It ain't been counted yet, but I'd say it's the biggest haul we ever made."

"At least six thousand," Frank said, studying their back-trail for dust sign along the horizon. "We ain't had no bad information yet."

"It's worth givin' up a share," Bob said.

Raymond's mouth drew into a thin line before he spoke on the subject of shares. "We got two to spare, since Carl an' Jimmy got killed. Seems a damn shame they had to die."

Frank gave Raymond Polk a stare. "Every man in this outfit knows the odds against him. A man robbin' trains is liable to get his head blowed off. I'd say we was lucky to get out with the money only losin' two men. You're gettin' soft, Raymond."

"Maybe," Raymond replied. "I was close to Jimmy all these years."

"Wasn't nobody close to Carl Hardin," Bob said, resting both palms on his saddlehorn. "He was a damn fool, the way he rode at Huling straight on."

Lefty wagged his head. "I ain't superstitious or nothin' like that, boys, but I say we quit talkin' about them that's dead an' get across this river."

Frank nodded his agreement, and urged his horse off the bluff above the Rio Grande. They had to be careful to avoid shifting quicksand beds here, but the water was low and several of his men carried ropes to drag trapped horses out if they got stuck in the sands.

Guarding their rear, Cotton Polk and Josh Walker kept an eye on the bleak, dry prairies they'd ridden to get to the border. Frank made sure Cotton and Josh were watching the brushlands before he kicked his horse down to the river.

"We ain't seen a soul all day," Lefty said, sending his bay into the shallows. "Not so much as a goat or a damn sheep."

"Seen a few buzzards circlin'," Bob remarked, "an' plenty of goddamn rattlesnakes."

"There'll be two-legged rattlers behind us," Frank said at the moment his horse entered the water. He grinned in spite of the pain from his festering wounds. "A hundred yards more an' them sons of bitches can't follow us. A thirsty man is mighty damn glad to find a river, if he does, but a man who's runnin' from the law ain't never seen no prettier sight that this muddy trickle. Same as sproutin' wings when the law's behind us."

Lefty frowned. "A bounty hunter don't have to stop, Frank. That railroad's liable to hire some real manhunters to come after this much money."

"We done killed Cletus Huling, an' we'll do the same to any other son of a bitch who makes a play for this loot. Soon as we get to Piedras Negras we're safe as a titty baby in his momma's arms."

"You gonna look for a doctor before then . . . when we ride to Acuna?" Bob asked.

"Ain't got much choice, Bob. I'm gonna die of blood poisoning if I don't." As he said it, he wondered if some members of his gang were hoping he *would* die from poisoned blood. That way, there would be another share to divide among them. He'd have to make sure he didn't turn his back on most of them, the ones he wasn't sure he could trust. Bob and Lefty were good men, and the Polk brothers would stand by him. But the rest were capable of shooting a man while he slept if the stakes were high enough, and the stakes were certainly high now, with so much money tied to their horses.

In most places the river was only belly-deep on their horses, and only once were the animals required to swim a short distance. Riding out on the other side, now safely in Mexico, Frank cast a glance back toward Texas. No one was following them.

"We made it!" Cotton cried, as his sorrel shook water

from its coat. "Yahoo! An' hooray for the Texas an' Pacific Railroad Company!"

Clyde Devers nodded, patting one sack stuffed with money tied to his saddlehorn. "They sure have been generous," he said, grinning.

Frank swung his horse in the direction of Villa Acuna, a sleepy Mexican border town to the untrained eye. But there was a *federale* garrison southeast of town with a hard headed commander, Porfirio Valdez. The old soldier wouldn't take a bribe, *la mordida,* from bandits crossing the river. When bounty hunters showed up looking for wanted men and stolen property, Valdez was all too willing to put them on an outlaw's trail without asking or taking a dime of reward money. It would be a bad idea to let Comandante Valdez know they were passing through Villa Acuna.

"Let's ride, boys," Frank said as the sun dropped below the horizon. He wondered if the wounds to his arm and shoulder were worth the risk of being caught by Valdez when he sought out a Mexican doctor.

The old man used a slender, pointed knife to dig out the pellets beneath Frank's skin. Then he seared each wound with a hot piece of thin wire. Frank flinched some when the doctor put the knife or the heated wire to work on him.

"Only a few more, Señor," he said.

Frank drank more tequila "Make it quick, Doc. You're bein' paid real well to do this right an' do it in a hurry."

"I understand, Señor. I do this as quick as I can, but it must be done correctly."

Lefty and Bob were with the money. Raymond and Sonny Jones were standing guard outside the little adobe building at the edge of the village while Cotton and Clyde went to a *mercado,* a market, to buy tortillas and limes and more tequila. They hadn't sighted any *federales* when they split up and rode quietly into town, but word of their arrival would surely reach the garrison soon, and Frank knew they were running out of time.

By the light of several candles, Dr. Gomez finished with the last of the angry red wounds, and covered it with a touch of pungent salve smelling of wintergreen. "This should do it," he said, standing back to inspect his work before he pulled down Frank's blood-encrusted shirtsleeve.

Frank got out of the straight-backed chair and took forty dollars in gold coins from his denims. "This is for what you did for me, an' to buy silence, old man. Don't say nothin' to nobody about doctorin' on no gringo tonight."

"I understand, Señor."

"In particular, I don't want no mention of it round the *comandante*."

"My lips are sealed," Gomez replied, pocketing the money. "I saw no Americanos here tonight. I saw nothing."

"*Gracias,*" Frank said as Gomez snuffed out the candles. The outlaw walked over to the door and peered cautiously outside.

"All clear, Boss," Sonny said, keeping an eye on the dark village. "Cotton's on his way back from the store an' he's got two tow sacks slung over his saddle, so I reckon we'll eat an' have some tequila."

"Get mounted," Frank said, eyeing the mesquite grove where Bob and Lefty waited with the loot. "Tell Cotton an' Clyde to skirt wide of town. We'll all join up where that road forks to the southeast. Make damn sure everybody rides quiet when we go south of that *federale* post. We ride that same arroyo we always do, so won't nobody be able to skyline us in the dark an' it'll keep any dogs from barkin'."

Silently, Frank and Raymond and Sonny walked around to the back of the adobe to mount their tethered horses. Even as much as the searing hot wire had hurt his arm, he was glad to have the last pellets removed from his hide.

Saddle leather creaked in the night as all three men

swung up. Cotton and Clyde had already reined off into the brush to avoid being seen by anyone in the tiny adobe huts clustered in this poorer section of town.

Frank led them into the mesquite grove where Bob and Lefty waited with the money. Josh Walker and Wilson Giles had just arrived. Frank turned to ask a question of Cotton, after a silent nod from Lefty told him things were okay. "Did anybody at the store pay particular attention to you?" he asked.

Cotton shook his head. "Did just like you said, Frank. I gave the storekeeper a ten-dollar gold piece to forget he ever seen us. He acted mighty damn glad to have the money, an' he throwed in some extra tortillas an' limes."

Frank scanned the blackened brushlands south of Villa Acuna before he rode out of the trees. "Don't see nobody about. But ride slow, like we ain't in no particular hurry. We'll head due south till we strike that draw."

Bob threw a glance over his shoulder as they were leaving the mesquites. "Didn't hear no dogs bark or nothin'. Looks like we'll get in an' out without no trouble."

"Don't be too damn sure," Frank warned, guiding his horse around a bed of prickly-pear cactus. "We ain't past that *federale* fort yet."

"I ain't gonna rest easy till we are," Lefty remarked, riding up beside Frank. "Last thing we need is to get in a shootout with a bunch of Meskin soldiers."

The bottom of the ravine was powder dry, winding its way to the east where it would eventually meet the Rio Grande. It had not rained in this part of Mexico for some time, Frank thought, as their horses sent up a telltale cloud of dust that would have been easy to spot in daylight.

Now and then an iron horseshoe clicked on a rocky spot, but for the most part their passage along the arroyo was as quiet as possible. Frank was beginning to feel a little better, for they should be passing below the *federale* garrison now, about a mile to the south.

But it was a part of Frank's nature to be careful at all times, and he still rode cautiously, holding the stud that once belonged to Carl Hardin in a steady walk. He watched the brush for any movement, cocking an ear to listen for the slightest sound that did not belong out here after dark.

It was Lefty Sikes who spotted the trouble first—he threw up his hand to halt their silent procession. "Look yonder, Boss, an' tell me if that's a rider headed across our path, way off to the south."

Frank stood in his stirrups to look over the lip of the dry wash. "Sure 'nough is," he whispered. "Just one is all I can see." He turned around in the saddle to speak to Josh Walker, for one of Josh's favorite weapons in a close-quarters fight was a Bowie knife. "You an' Clyde ride down this ravine ahead of us an' if it's a *federale* soldier, kill him. Use your knife if you get the chance. We can't have him ridin' back to the fort to say he seen a bunch of Americanos out here at night. The *comandante* will know it ain't usual, an' he's liable to send a patrol hot on our heels. If you kill the guy yonder, they won't find him till daylight tomorrow an' nobody'll know it was us who done it. If we're lucky, they'll figure he got robbed. Take his guns an' empty his pockets so it'll look like a robbery."

"They'll find our tracks, come daylight," Raymond said, "an' they could follow us all the way down to Piedras Negras."

"We're gonna take care of that, soon as we get past the fort where this draw meets the river. We'll ride in the river a ways so we don't leave no tracks."

"If that's a *federale,* we can toss his body in the river too an' that way he'll float plumb to Laredo," Josh said. "We'll take his horse with us. Won't be nothin' for that *comandante* to find, that way."

"Just get it done," Frank said.

Josh and Clyde rode quietly past the others, staying down in the arroyo until they went out of sight around a bend.

"Hope there don't have to be no shootin'," Bob said, "or somebody's liable to hear it."

Frank waited, impatient with the delay, drinking tequila to steady his nerves. Like the others, he sure as hell didn't want a running gun battle with a troop of *federales*.

Twenty minutes later he heard a soft cry in the distance.

"Josh got him with the blade," Lefty said. "We ain't had nothin' but good luck lately."

Frank led his men forward along the arroyo, thinking the same thing about their recent good fortune. The real key to their success lay in knowing which train to rob, and that was what made all the difference.

12

The locomotive labored up a series of winding turns to cross a range of steep rock hills. Slocum rode in a modified passenger car with crewmen who would repair the damage at Devil's River Canyon and salvage what they could from wrecked railroad cars. A cool breeze scented with smoke from the engine passed through windows while the train chugged steadily westward. A crew chief for the Texas and Pacific sat beside Slocum. They talked occasionally and smoked cigars.

"I've got it figured another way," Charlie Waters said, as he stared out a window at empty rangeland. "Them robbers know when there's money aboard, so you start with who's sendin' the money to figure out how Clanton is wise to the schedule. Makes it the army where this information comes from. Some soldier at Fort Sam is buildin' himself a little nest egg for when he up an' retires."

It was, Slocum knew, a strong possibility. "Colonel Bush told me he's checked every angle at the fort," he said. "Questioned every man who knows ahead of time when the payroll is going out. The information needs time to reach Clanton, so he can cross over the border and set up a place to derail the train, and Clanton also has to do it so the handcar crew from Pandale doesn't find it when they do their weekly run through Devil's River Canyon on Wednesday, which is when Willard Clifton said no trains pass along that line from either direction. Somebody has to fix an obstacle on the rails at just the right time, so the wrong train won't jump the tracks. They have to know exactly when to do it. That could come from the railroad . . . someone Clifton told about it. I don't think he's in on it himself. The third possibility is that the president of the Planters Bank talks to somebody, maybe unintentionally, and word goes by wire or a messenger down to Clanton. It can be happening any one of those three ways.''

Charlie, a man of fifty wearing greasy overalls, puffed on his cigar thoughtfully. He'd been with the Texas and Pacific for eleven years, he'd said. "It *could* be somebody with the railroad, I reckon. Like you, I don't figure Mr. Clifton has anything to do with it. I never seen a man act so scared of losin' his job. But when he tells the yard foreman to bring a baggage car with one of them big safes to a certain sidin' with the little switch engine, every man workin' in the yard knows what day that baggage car will be coupled with passenger an' boxcars for the El Paso run. Just seein' which side track that special baggage car is on tells any man who works around the yards what day it'll leave an' which direction it's goin'.''

Slocum hadn't considered this, or known the routine existed. A spotter who worked for any of the rail lines passing through San Antone would be able to send word to Clanton that a certain kind of baggage car was waiting on a side track where a train bound for El Paso on a certain day was being assembled. "I had wondered about someone watching the office, like when this same Sergeant Baker rides up to inform Clifton that a payroll is going out one week later, but I hadn't thought about the side track being a dead giveaway. You say it's always the same siding for a particular day?''

"Only way we got to get the right cars together for whatever train is booked for that run. We run our northeast line seven days a week. Six days southwest, on account of ain't much in the way of passenger traffic, usually . . . not comin' from San Antone to El Paso, there ain't.''

"I didn't know," Slocum said. "Any man who works in the rail yards could be the source of information to Clanton. Send a wire to him telling him something about Thursday, for instance, or Monday. Could be coded, more or less. Clanton gets the wire at the Mexican border, and he knows what day the payroll is headed for Devil's River Canyon."

"I only said it *could* be happenin' that way," Charlie explained.

The way things stood, there were too many possibilities, in Slocum's view. Digging out the connection to Clanton was going to be tough.

The car rocked and swayed around a curve toward a red ball of setting sun. Clifton had said the engineer could get them to the site of the robbery by tomorrow morning, without any mechanical problems or unforseen delays, if they pushed the locomotive hard with a light load of flatcars. Slocum wanted to get there ahead of the army and the Rangers if he could.

The train began to descend a long grade, picking up speed. It was beginning to look like this investigation would turn out to be far more complicated than he'd first guessed. Malcom Warren was paying all expenses and a generous fee to find out what the hell was going on in his San Antonio operation, and Slocum owed it to him, because of a long-standing friendship as well as for the money, to do everything he could to get to the bottom of these robberies, perhaps even get this latest stolen payroll back if he could.

His bay stud climbed down a loading ramp, looking to be in good shape after riding in the cattle car. Before Slocum saddled the horse, he'd inspected the site of the wreckage. A locomotive lay on its side, charred metal twisted, wheels broken off on one side, and with a ruptured boiler. Blackened brush all around the wrecked locomotive showed how large the explosion and fire had been when the boiler ruptured.

What was left of the baggage car was little more than a flat platform littered with bent metal and splintered wood. The cast-iron safe, what remained of it, lay on its back with its door blasted away.

"Dynamite, and plenty of it," Charlie had said when they first got off the train to inspect the baggage car and the safe. Then he'd led some of his crewmen along the tracks.

Slocum was inspecting one missing rail just east of a wooden bridge when Charlie walked back and spoke to him.

"Had to get 'em started," he said.

Two men on a handcar were talking to other members of the repair crew where a passenger car and several boxcars had left the track. Men had begun unloading new rails and cross-ties using pulleys and ropes to get them off flatcars. Charlie had seen to the commencement of repairs before he came over to see what Slocum was up to.

"The spikes were pulled where this rail used to be," Slocum said. "Not one is twisted off or laying bent somewhere near the track. Clanton pulled them out before the train got here, so the weight of the engine would push it over and send the locomotive off to the side here. The rest of the cars followed until their couplings broke off."

Charlie frowned, examining holes in the cross-ties where all the spikes were missing. "Appears you're right, Mr. Slocum. I'd been lookin' around for somethin' they piled across the tracks to derail it."

Slocum cast a glance to the south, toward the Mexican border—seventy or eighty miles away, by the map he carried. "I'll start looking for their trail. When you wire Mr. Clifton, tell him I'll see where Clanton crossed into Mexico . . . maybe do a little bit of nosing around down there. I could be gone a week or two, depending. And while you're at it, ask him to inform Mr. Warren at the Fort Worth office what I'll be doing. I'm sure your men will be busy, but Mr. Clifton and Mr. Warren need to know what we found so far.''

''It'll take us nearly a week to clear this wreck an' get the rails back in shape. I'll ask somebody to pump that handcar to Fort Stockton so a wire can be sent to the San Antone office. I'll be sure an' tell Mr. Clifton what you said about sendin' a wire to Fort Worth.''

Slocum tightened the cinch on his stallion and stepped into a stirrup to mount. ''I'll send a wire from Del Rio or wherever the hoofprints take me. Could swing most any direction . . . if I can find them at all, which I figure I will.''

Charlie frowned up at him. ''You sure don't dress like no tracker, Mr. Slocum. Ain't wearin' the right clothes to be off in wild dry country. Just lookin' at you, I'd have said you was a city type.''

''I've got a change in my saddlebags. Besides, I never judge what another man is capable of by looking at him. Can't always tell, that way.'' He grinned at Charlie and swung over a saddle burdened with his bedroll and saddle-bags, his Winchester .44 rifle, and two canteens, since he'd be crossing desert country most of the way to the border.

''Good luck,'' Charlie said as Slocum made to ride off. ''An' keep an eye over your shoulder.''

''I always do,'' Slocum replied, touching heels to his horse to begin a careful search for hoofprints in the caliche soil and rock. He would ride widening circles until he found horse sign somewhere to the south.

The trail of almost a dozen horses was easy to find in brush not far south of the rail line. And in places he found blood, a few drops here and there.

''One of 'em's wounded,'' he told himself, pausing long enough to read messages left in the caliche.

The hoofprints led almost due south, the shortest route to the Rio Grande. He urged his long-gaited thoroughbred to a lope, for this trail would be easy to follow . . . until it got dark.

A warm wind blew from the west as his horse sent up swirls of yellow-white dust from its hooves. To an experienced eye it would be announcing his presence. But by now, Slocum was certain, the outlaws were in Mexico, perhaps already enjoying the fruits of their ill-gotten gains. If he could find them, the celebration might not last as long as they'd figured.

Circling buzzards warned of death somewhere up ahead. Slocum slowed his horse from a ground-eating trot to a walk, removing the hammer thong holding his Colt .44/.40 in its holster. A wounded outlaw could be waiting in ambush for him somewhere in the brush, or a man who'd simply lost a horse to a rattlesnake bite or a broken leg after stepping in a gopher hole. The last possibility was a wounded or dead horse abandoned by the gang, but it always paid to be careful.

The vultures swooped down into an arroyo now and then, to guide him to the spot where death smell attracted them from the skies. Slocum approached the ravine cautiously with his pistol drawn, halting the stud every now and then to allow his senses to warn him of trouble.

Fifty yards farther down the arroyo, he saw what had the buzzards gathered. The body of a man lay sprawled in the meager shade of a mesquite tree. Blood had pooled around him, drying in the afternoon sun.

The bay snorted. "Easy, boy," he said quietly. "He ain't gonna put up any fight . . . lost too much blood." It appeared the man was dead, until Slocum rode closer, noticing a slight rise and fall of the man's chest.

He swung down and ground-hitched his stud before walking up to the mesquite. Ants had already swarmed around the body to feed on the blood. Slocum holstered his gun and went over for a look at the man's face. Dozens of pulpy shotgun wounds covered his cheeks and chest. A heavily charged scattergun shell had struck him at close range.

Slocum swatted away swarms of blowflies to grab the front of the man's shirt, dragging him away from the blood and ants to a yucca plant providing some shade.

When he felt himself being moved, the man's eyes fluttered open briefly.

"I'll get you some water," Slocum told him, certain the man would die soon, yet unwilling to leave him thirsty in his final hour. As he turned to fetch down a canteen, he asked, "Where is Frank headed? Where is Mexico? I need to find him real quick and give him some bad news."

"You . . . the . . . law?" the man croaked.

"No. I'm not the law. Honest."

"Piedras . . . Piedras Negras. Same . . . as before. Never . . . did think . . . they'd leave . . . me like this."

"I'll get that water," Slocum said, heading for his horse. The dying outlaw had given him an important scrap of information. Piedras Negras was far to the southeast, across the Rio Grande from Eagle Pass in Texas. It was easy enough to figure. Clanton had connections in Piedras Negras, or a safe hiding place. He was throwing off pursuit by private bounty hunters by crossing over into Mexico at the closest place, then most likely moving downriver on the Mexican side until he reached his hideout. It would save Slocum precious time to ride the river as fast as he could without worrying about losing the tracks. He might make it to Piedras Negras right behind Clanton and his men.

He returned to the yucca plant too late to offer the outlaw a last sip of water. Death had claimed him, and even the buzzards seemed to know, for they fluttered heavily to the ground not far from the body, as if waiting for Slocum to leave so they could begin their grisly meal.

He walked back to the stud, hanging his canteen over the saddlehorn before he mounted. Turning his gaze to the east, he figured he would have to guess at the right direction until he reached Del Rio, across the Rio Grande from Villa

Acuna. There, he'd pay a call on Comandante Porfirio Valdez, just to let him know about Clanton and his gang being in Mexico, although it was possible Valdez was no longer in charge of the *federale* garrison. It had been years since Slocum was in Acuna, back when he'd gone after a horse thief and a pretty woman who'd thought the river would keep them safe from John Slocum's wrath.

13

A game trail wandered through the brush, and Slocum knew it would take him to the river, for even deer and javelina pigs and other desert creatures had to have water. Riding in moonlight, he let the horse pick its own way and use its keen senses to detect rattlers crossing the path. To pass time while he covered empty miles, he recalled his first night in San Antone in the arms of lovely Rose Miller. She was one of those rare beauties he was sure he would remember the rest of his life. Her passion equaled his own in bed, and though he'd had his share of passionate women, few could compare with Rose in that category. It was unusual to find so much beauty and lust in one package.

Be a shame if she turned out to be in cahoots with Clanton, he thought, hoping for another chance to experience her charms before he left this part of the state.

Another regret would be leaving Claire behind. In her own innocent way, she was as delightful as Rose Miller, though much more reluctant at first. That night on the riverbank, she'd found ways to satisfy him only more experienced women understood. She was an eager student, with ample charms of her own and a lust for lovemaking that took control of her, aided by a bottle of peach brandy.

Something alerted his horse . . . its neck bowed and it let

out a soft rattle from its muzzle, slowing its strides. He
stood in the stirrups to see what lay ahead, or around him.

Then he saw it, a huge rattlesnake slithering across the
game trail, as thick as a man's arm and close to six feet in
length.

"Now there's a killer," he whispered, pulling the stud
to a halt. He would let it pass for like all of nature's creatures, it had a purpose. The trouble was, too many times
the rattler's temperment made it too dangerous to leave
alive when it was near a settlement where an inexperienced
person or a child might be bitten.

The giant snake crawled out of sight into the brush, and
still he waited a moment, to be sure it was far enough from
the trail to keep it from striking his horse.

"A man on foot in this country's as good as dead," he
said, as if speaking to the horse underneath him.

Half a minute later Slocum was moving again, crossing
some of the emptiest land on earth . . . and the driest. His
canteens would keep him and his horse alive until they
reached the Rio Grande.

For hours, holding a steady trot, the bay carried him
south and east. At night the air was cooler, easier on horses,
and he judged he was making good time. Aboard a good
traveling horse, he expected to reach Del Rio before sunrise.

He pulled a bottle of Kentucky sour-mash whiskey from
his saddlebags and wet his throat with a bubbling swallow.
Then he lit a cigar with a lucifer he scratched across his
saddlehorn and settled back against the cantle of his saddle,
blowing sweet smoke into the night air. At times like this
he actually enjoyed himself out in open spaces, no matter
how harsh the land might be.

Soon enough, if he found Frank Clanton and the army's
payroll money in Piedras Negras, where the dying outlaw
had said it and Clanton's gang would be, all forms of en-
joyment would be over and the serious business of getting
the money back would begin.

• • •

He rode through Del Rio on his way across the Rio Grande as false dawn brightened the eastern skies. An elderly man aboard a red sorrel mule was about to make the low-water crossing just when Slocum rode down to the river. At this early hour the streets were virtually empty.

"Headed fer Acuna?" the man asked, though the answer was so obvious. He wore faded denims and a battered straw hat, and his shirt had holes in both elbows. Clay jugs wrapped in burlap were tied behind his old cavalry saddle, and Slocum supposed he was heading across the river to fill his jugs with tequila, or pulque.

"That's right," Slocum replied, guiding his stallion into the soft mud along the river's edge.

"What brings you? I can see you're a traveler. You ain't from these parts an' it sure is early for folks to be headin' to Mexico, 'less they's on business."

Slocum decided to fish for some information. "Headed over to see an old friend of mine, if he's still there, a Comandante Porfirio Valdez. He used to be in charge of the *federale* garrison."

"Still is," the old man remarked. His mule seemed reluctant to enter the river until Slocum's stud led the way. "I'm acquainted with him. Tell him Elmer Dodd says howdy-do when you git out to the post."

"I'll give him your regards, Mr. Dodd."

Dodd urged his mule up beside Slocum. "Couldn't help but notice you carry a six-shooter in a cross-draw rig like you's a gunfighter by trade."

"I'm not a hired gun. It's just my way. Got used to it a long time back and can't change my ways."

"Most shootists claim it's too slow to pull a gun across the belly."

"I never did claim to be the fastest."

"You watch out fer them that's fast over yonder in Mexico, stranger. In case you didn't know, there's some bad men over that side."

Slocum wondered if Dodd knew about the train robbery, or if he knew Clanton by name. "You mean gents like Frank Clanton, the train robber?" Slocum offered.

"You damn right that's the type I'm talkin' about. Clanton don't hang round Villa Acuna on account of your friend Valdez. Comandante Valdez makes it mighty hard on criminals an' hardcases from the other side who figure to hide in his jurisdiction. He runs most of 'em out of town."

"I'll feel safer," Slocum replied, "now that you've told me Clanton isn't in Villa Acuna. "Where does he go if he isn't welcome here?"

"Some say he stays in Nuevo Laredo, when he ain't up north robbin' trains or banks, but I got better information on him."

"How's that, Mr. Dodd?"

" 'Cause I know a feller who seen him down in Piedras Negras lots of times. Hangs around this place called the Agave Cantina, an' it's a hangout fer bad hombres, so I hear tell. Clanton is one of the worst, they claim."

Slocum's horse neared the middle of the river. "I'm much obliged for the warning, Mr. Dodd. I'll stay as far away from Piedras Negras as I can."

Dodd shook his head. "You'll live a helluva lot longer if you do, stranger. Like I said, nearly every shootist knows a cross-draw rig like yours is way too slow, goin' up against a feller like Frank Clanton, Bob Walls, or Lefty Sikes."

Slocum turned in the saddle. "Are those some of the men who ride with Clanton?"

Again, Dodd nodded. "Watch out fer them too. Lefty Sikes is real quick on the trigger. Bob Walls is every damn bit as good, so folks say."

"I'll keep those two names in mind. You've been very helpful. Thanks again."

Slocum heeled his horse to a trot when shallow water would allow it, thinking about what the old man told him. He'd never heard of Lefty Sikes or Bob Walls, but that wouldn't have made a difference anyway. Names were of little importance until they were needed by an undertaker to have them carved into a marker for a grave.

Riding slowly down the main road through Villa Acuna, he saw a woman setting up a small cart with a sign on it, offering him just what he needed for breakfast, tamales and tortillas. She was just about the only person moving about in Acuna before the sun came up.

He stopped his horse at the woman's cart and asked for both tamales and corn tortillas. She smiled and took paper packages from the bottom of her cart, handing them up to Slocum.

He gave her a few silver coins and rode off, leaving the old woman with surprise written all over her face. The food he'd bought was probably only worth a few pesos and he'd given her far too much money, but as hungry as he was, the difference was of no consequence.

Unwrapping a corn shuck around a juicy tamale, still warm from the oven, he bit into a delicious mix of ground meat and corn paste. Seconds later his mouth began to burn from all the peppers, and he reached for a canteen to cool down the chilis sizzling on his tongue.

"Sure is good," he mumbled around another mouthful. "Hot as hell, but mighty damn good to a hungry man who's been in a saddle all day and all night."

The small *federale* fort was enclosed by an adobe wall, and when he rode to the gate a pair of soldiers blocked his path into the compound.

"I'm here to see Comandante Porfirio Valdez," he said, with the hope they understood English. It had been years since he'd used any of the Spanish he knew, and even at that, his vocabulary was severely limited.

"You wait, Americano," one of the soldiers said.

"I'll wait," Slocum replied, slumped in the saddle, worn down by the long ride.

The soldier hurried off while the other kept a wary eye

on Slocum, cradling an old musket in the crook of his arm. And he paid particular attention to the rifle booted to Slocum's saddle and the pistol at his waist.

Dawn came full to the brushlands beside the Rio Grande, and its light gave the desert a false beauty, hiding thousands of sharp thorns and cactus needles. In a way it was pretty, but not the sort of place where Slocum wanted to live. Cool mountains and tall pines were more to his liking.

Several minutes later the guard came out of an adobe building with a barrel-chested man dressed in a dark blue uniform with red trim on the sleeves and trousers. A shock of unruly gray hair did not hide the features on Porfirio Valdez's deeply wrinkled face.

Slocum swung down from the saddle and thumbed back his hat, smiling when he recognized his old friend. *"Comandante,"* he said as he held out his hand. "John Slocum. It's been a few years, I reckon."

The *comandante*'s face broke into a broad smile. "Ah, yes, it is you, Señor Slocum . . . the gringo with the very deadly guns. It is good to see you again." He took Slocum's palm and pumped his hand. "Come inside. We must talk and drink coffee while you tell me where you have been and why you are here."

"I'm afraid the reason I'm here won't be good news," he said as one soldier took the reins of the bay stud.

Valdez halted in mid-stride as they were walking toward the main building inside the adobe wall. He gave Slocum a questioning look. "And why is that, my friend?"

"I'm looking for a gang of holdup men, a gang of ten or twelve who rob trains."

"Train robbers? Here in Villa Acuna? I would not tolerate such a thing."

"I know. I followed their tracks most of the way to the Rio Grande. I've heard from two sources they hide out down in the village of Piedras Negras."

Valdez nodded, as though the news did not surprise him. "It is very small, too small for but a few soldiers under the command of Capitan Vela. I have heard that Capitan Vela will . . . look the other way when wanted men from the north are in his village. I have been told this.''

"I've got to try to find these holdup men,'' Slocum said, following Valdez into a big dining room. There a younger soldier was tending to a fire in a wood stove where a pot of coffee was on to boil.

"Sit down, amigo,'' Valdez said, pointing to a table where benches were lined up on either side to feed soldiers. "I will bring coffee and I will tell you as much as I can.'' He grinned again. "You I will never forget, John Slocum. I have never in all my life seen one man who was so good with guns, a man who has no fear.''

Slocum merely shrugged when he heard the compliment, and sat down.

"That was many years ago, perhaps five or six or seven,'' the *comandante* continued as the soldier poured two tin cups of steaming coffee.

"The years may have changed me,'' Slocum replied. "I may be too old for what I'm gonna try to do.''

"And what is this you will try to do?'' Valdez asked, placing a cup in front of Slocum.

"I'm gonna try to get six thousand American dollars back for a friend of mine who runs a railroad up in Texas. It was on a train that was robbed a few days ago, and the outlaws brought it to Mexico.''

Valdez scowled before he took his seat opposite Slocum. "But you say there may be ten or twelve of these bad hombres?''

"That's what I was told, and that's about the right number of horse tracks I followed down here.''

"Is too many for one man,'' Valdez warned, ignoring his cup of coffee for now.

Slocum blew steam from his cup. "I never was one to worry too much about the odds. Tell me what you know about the lay of things around Piedras Negras, and this Capitan Vela, just in case I have dealings with him.''

"Of course, amigo." The *comandante* hesitated, scowling. "One of my soldiers is missing on night patrol last night. He did not come back and we can find no trace of him. I am wondering if this has something to do with the train robbers you are after."

"It's quite possible," Slocum said. "I'm told these are real hardcases."

14

Frank put his right arm around the Mexican girl's slender waist. A guitar played softly in a corner of the Agave Cantina while he and his men drank tequila and chewed salted limes.

"What's your name, Señorita?" he asked, pulling her down on his lap.

"Carmen," she said softly, fluttering her long eyelashes, smiling at him.

"That's a right pretty name. I'm gonna give you two whole dollars in American silver to take me back to one of them rooms an' hump my ears off."

The girl blushed. "I am new with this, Señor. I have just come to the north of Mexico from Michoacan. I . . . need money very much. I no speak much English. I no . . . how you say? Sell me for money?"

Bob Walls, seated across the table from Frank, laughed. "You got a brand-new whore, Frank. If you want, I'll break her in for you."

Frank studied Carmen's youthful figure. Her breasts swelled above the top of a low-cut homespun cotton blouse. A simple tan skirt hid the shape of her legs and the roundness of her hips. "I believe I'll do the job myself, Bob. She needs to be broke in just right."

Bob chuckled again. "Don't do no damage, Boss. I may want to buy her later on tonight."

Frank saw a hint of fear in the girl's eyes. "She's stayin' with me," he told Bob. "I can tell I'm gonna like teachin' her a few tricks."

Carmen glanced at his bandaged arm and shoulder. "You hurt bad?" she asked.

"Not bad enough to keep me from bangin' you, darlin'. I've had worse."

"This money you pay me . . . is how much?"

"Two silver dollars. That's more'n some *peon* makes workin' in a cornfield down here in a month. You're gonna make it all in one night, only you'd better do just like I say. When I tell you to put my cock in your mouth, you'd goddamn sure better do it an' do it gentle."

"What is . . . cock?"

He pointed down to his crotch, grinning.

Carmen looked away. "I never do this thing," she said, embarrassed.

"You'll learn. Now go fetch me a bowl of them beans an' a pile of tortillas from the kitchen out back. An' don't be gone too damn long."

"*Sí, Señor.*" She got up quickly and hurried across a dirt floor, disappearing into a room off the back.

Frank turned to Raymond at a nearby table. "Ride out to the hut an' take Lefty a girl an' somethin' to eat. Pick out a real pretty whore. Don't forget to take him more tequila. Wouldn't want him to get too lonely, standin' guard all by himself with nothin' but that money for company."

Raymond grinned and got out of his chair. He stopped at Frank's table. "We gonna divide it up first thing in the mornin'?"

"Same as always. After we get done countin' it out real good, we cut it into shares. Ain't gonna do it no different this time."

Raymond nodded. "Kinda makes me nervous, all that money in a damn hole in the floor. Sure do hope nobody

knows about it an' jumps Lefty while he's humpin' one of
these gals. I could take a whore out there fer me, an' Cotton
could take one along so's we could stay with Lefty till
mornin'. That way, there'd be three of us."

It occurred to Frank that Raymond and his brother might
be planning to jump Lefty themselves and run out on the
others with all the loot. Six thousand dollars was enough
money to make men turn on each other, though he hadn't
expected it to come from Raymond or Cotton. The offer
Raymond made sounded suspicious as hell, and he still
acted a little sore about leaving Jimmy Ballard behind. If
one of the Polk brothers got behind Lefty while he was
occupied with a Mexican whore, it would be all too easy
to kill him, even a man as cautious as Lefty. Bob and Lefty
were the two men Frank really trusted. "Just go by yourself
with one of them whores. That adobe hut ain't got but one
door, an' Lefty can keep an eye on it while he's humpin'.
Ride on back soon as you get it done. Hell, we're havin'
ourselves a damn celebration here. Wouldn't want you or
Cotton to miss it."

Raymond gave a silent nod and went over to the bar
where a dark-eyed girl stood watching the Americans. He
took her by the arm and spoke to the bartender.

Bob Walls lowered his voice before Carmen approached
their table with a bowl of beans and a platter of tortillas.
"You got somethin' on your mind, ain't you, Frank? You
figure Raymond an' Cotton is plannin' to double-cross us,
maybe?"

"It crossed my mind. Raymond was too damn quick to
offer to take Cotton along. The two of 'em could jump
Lefty if he wasn't suspectin' nothin'."

Bob frowned. "Them Polk boys been with us quite a
spell, Frank."

"An' six thousand dollars is a hell of a lot of money,"
Frank replied, watching Raymond tuck a bottle of tequila
under his arm, then take a sack of tortillas and the girl
toward the front door of the Agave. "Help me keep an eye

on Cotton. If he so much as goes out back to piss, follow him out there. Raymond ain't been actin' right since we had to leave Jimmy. Maybe him an' his brother hatched up the idea to rob the rest of us after we got drunk tonight.''

Bob was watching Raymond too, until Raymond walked out of the bat-wing doors with the whore. "Maybe we oughta split up for a spell, Frank," he said softly. "Lay low after we divide the loot between us. You an' me an' Lefty could stay together while the rest go wherever it suits 'em. Stayin' together draws attention to us.''

"I'd thought about breakin' up the gang," Frank agreed as Carmen gave him his food. "It'll be too dangerous to go back to that canyon for a long time. They'll be watchin' it too close, expectin' it to happen again. No real reason for us to stay in one bunch now. We've all got plenty of money, enough to last us a year or more down here." He pulled the girl back into his lap and reached for a bottle of tequila. "We could agree to meet up again some place . . . maybe this cantina a year from now. Then we could hit that railroad again. They'll figure we went somewheres else.''

"Less likely some of our own bunch would get greedy," Bob said. "I'll go along with whatever you say.''

Frank wondered about the money tonight, after what Raymond had said on his way out. Were the Polk brothers, maybe with one or two more, planning a double cross? The money was buried in a pit in the dirt floor of a two-room adobe hut they'd rented from an old goatherder, a crumbling ruin without much furniture and with a few holes in the roof. But it was a good place to defend on the edge of Piedras Negras if something went wrong, sitting out in an open pasture with no cover on all four sides, perfect to keep anyone from slipping up on the place unseen. And Capitan Vela knew they were there. He'd been well paid to keep anyone from bothering them or nosing around. Vela had six soldiers under his command, enough to discourage a bounty hunter or a railroad detective who might discover where they were hiding. Anyone who showed up in Piedras

Negras asking too many questions would wind up in the iron cage behind Vela's outpost headquarters or they might meet with an unfortunate accident.

Frank watched Cotton for any sign he intended to leave to join his brother, but Cotton had a chubby Mexican whore in his lap. He was laughing, playing with one of her breasts, and drinking tequila like the others, as if he had nothing else on his mind. Frank wondered if he was too edgy. Bob's idea made sense. He and Lefty and Bob could stay together after the money was split, and the others could go wherever the urge struck them. "I'll tell everybody tomorrow what we aim to do," Frank said. "The rest can ride off in different directions while the three of us stay here for a spell."

Bob shook his head. "Be smarter," he said, motioning to the barman to bring him another jug of tequila.

Frank turned his attention to Carmen. "Let's you an' me go to one of them rooms out back, darlin'. Got some money I want to give you, an' somethin' I want to show you."

The girl got up timidly, waiting for Frank to rise. Frank spoke to Bob before he headed to one of the whores' rooms. "You keep an eye on Cotton. Come get me if he leaves the cantina on a horse."

"It's same as done," Bob said, patting the handgrips on his Walker Colt .44.

"You've got a nice body," Frank whispered, kneading Carmen's left breast roughly. Tears trickled from the corners of her eyes. He'd slapped her once, when she'd shown reluctance to put his cock in her mouth, driving her back against the adobe mud wall of a tiny room furnished with a cot, a candle, and a small washstand with a pitcher of water on it. The candle had flickered in a breath of wind passing through the door to the room's only window. She'd taken his prick in her mouth and sucked on it when he'd pulled her up off the floor.

She lay on the cot naked now, while he played with her cunt and her breasts. He bit down on one nipple hard enough to draw a trace of blood, and yet the girl was wise enough not to protest, merely closing her eyes with the pain, gritting her teeth, a low moan coming from her throat.

His cock was rock-hard after that. It got harder when he inflicted pain on a whore. "Spread them legs, bitch," he said gruffly. "I'm gonna wallow out that hole you got so it won't be so damn tight."

Carmen opened her thighs for him, keeping her eyes tightly shut while he crawled between them.

"That's it, you rotten little whore!" he snarled, stabbing his cock into her mound. "How come you ain't wet, bitch? You want I should slap you again?"

"No. Please."

She spread her legs wider, and he found he could enter her without much difficulty. Then he began rocking back and forth with short, hard thrusts, making the rawhide webbing supporting the cornshuck mattress creak with each rapid movement.

"You like it, don't you, bitch?" he hissed, his beard-stubbled face pressed against her cheek. "Tell me you like it, you goddamn whore!"

"Me . . . like . . . it," she groaned, as more tears flooded down her face.

His jism rose quickly, for it had been weeks since he'd been with a woman. He slammed his prick into her cunt with all his might, nearing his release, sweating, panting, gripping the edge of the cot with one hand and Carmen's long black hair with the other.

"Señor . . . please," Carmen moaned, inching away from his stabbing thrusts toward the wall, until her head was bumping against it.

His balls exploded, and he grunted with pleasure as his seed spilled inside the girl. He collapsed on top of her with all his weight, breathing hard while the warm feeling melted away in his groin.

A moment later he heard Carmen sobbing. Rising up on his elbows, he looked at her. "What's the matter with you, bitch? Was my cock too big for you?'' After he said it, he laughed and loosened his grip on her hair.

The sound of spur rowels rattling over hard caliche came toward the doorway into his room. Out of old habit, he reached under the cot and jerked out his pistol.

"Frank, it's me."

He recognized Bob's voice. "What is it, Bob? Can't you see I'm in here fuckin' this girl?"

"You said you wanted to know if Cotton left the cantina. He just did."

Frank came flying off the mattress with his pants down around his knees, his gun clamped in his fist. "Which way'd he go?"

"I seen him ride off south with a jug of tequila. Means he's most likely headed out to the adobe."

"Damn them double-crossin' Polk brothers!" he bellowed, pulling up his denims, stomping into his boots. "Bring my horse around!"

He heard Bob hurrying off while he was buckling on his gunbelt. "The rotten, no-good bastards," he said, rage welling in his chest. He'd guessed right about the double cross right from the start.

Frank tossed two silver dollars on the cot where Carmen sat crying softly, one hand pressed to her cunt. "There's your damn money, whore!" he snapped, stalking through the open doorway to meet up with Bob.

He saw Bob's silhouette in the moonlight, leading the horse that once belonged to Carl Hardin. Frank broke into a trot to meet Bob at a corner of the cantina.

"You was right, Boss," Bob said as Frank climbed hurriedly into the saddle. "Sure does look like them Polks aim to kill Lefty an' take the money for themselves."

Frank's jaw clamped as he wheeled his horse around. "They ain't got it done yet. Let's ride!"

15

Galloping south out of town, Frank yelled to be heard above the rumble of running horses' hooves on hard dirt. "You skirt round to the back. I'll come from the front."

Bob nodded as they passed the last adobe hut at the outskirts of the village. Open desert lay in every direction, a few mesquites rising like fire-blackened skeleton fingers against a night sky. The hut they were riding for was less than half a mile from Piedras Negras, west of the road to Nava.

Frank loosed his rifle from its boot and levered a shell into the firing chamber, and when Bob saw what he was doing he pulled his own Winchester .44 and jacked a cartridge into place. In pale light from a piece of moon, the desert took on a curious glow as they raced toward their hideout, and the money.

Bob swung off the wagon road when he came to a goat trail leading into the brush. He rode out of sight into a tangle of brush and stunted mesquites.

A quarter mile farther south, Frank caught a glimpse of the adobe hideout. Three horses were tied to a hitching post out front, and he knew he'd probably been right to guess that Cotton would come here to help his brother rob Lefty and make off with the entire army payroll. Three horses meant Lefty and Raymond and Cotton were all inside, and Lefty most likely had no idea the brothers intended to kill him.

"Bastards," he said, slowing his horse to a trot, then down to a walk. He wanted to be sure he was just wide of good rifle range in the dark when he called out to Lefty, to find out if the Polk boys had already killed him or if they were merely holding him at gunpoint for now, until they got all the money out of the pit.

A shadow moved near the doorway, the outline of a man in a cowboy hat, and Frank was puzzled, jerking his horse to a complete stop. Lefty was standing in the doorway with a rifle balanced in the crook of his arm. He was still alive, and he still carried a gun. Could Frank have been wrong? Or had he simply gotten here in the nick of time.

"Who's out there?" It was Lefty's voice.

"It's me! Frank! Just rode out to make sure things was all right!"

"Never been no better. Plenty of tequila an' now we've got us a woman. How come you don't ride up?"

Frank hoped he and Bob had come just in time to keep Cotton and Raymond honest. Maybe they'd planned to kill Lefty after they got him drunk. But there was another possiblity . . . he and Bob might have been wrong all along to believe the Polk boys would turn on members of the gang. Still, things didn't quite add up. Why was Cotton here in the first place?

"You right sure there ain't nothin' wrong?" Frank asked again, listening closely for the tone of Lefty's reply and the words he used.

"Not a damn thing, Boss. How come you keep askin'?"

Maybe he'd jumped to conclusions, Frank thought. "Just bein' careful, is all." Resting the butt plate of his Winchester on his left knee, he spurred his horse toward the hut at a slow walk. Bob was out there somewhere, and Frank hoped he'd been listening to the conversation. If Bob suspected something was amiss, he'd hide out in the brush behind the house until Frank gave him a signal to ride in.

Frank was fifty yards from the house when he saw Raymond walk outside with a bottle in one hand. The other hand was empty. A girl giggled inside the hut. Through one glassless window he saw Cotton peer outside.

"That you, Boss?" Cotton yelled, sounding a bit drunk when his words ran together.

Frank relaxed his grip on the rifle. There was no hint that anything other than drinking and womanizing was going on inside the place, although this still didn't explain why Cotton had left the cantina to join his brother. "It's me," Frank called back, moving his horse forward again, although he had a nagging feeling there was something missing, or out of place, and the sensation became stronger as he neared the hut.

And then it happened, so suddenly he was caught off guard in spite of his earlier caution. A gun flashed in the window where Cotton Polk's head and shoulders were visible, followed by the crack of a pistol shot.

Lefty Sikes twisted, lurching forward away from the door in an instant. At the same time Raymond drew his gun and fired at Frank, three shots in succession. Speeding balls of molten lead whizzed past him, all three narrow misses.

Frank's horse reared on its hind legs, bawling, pawing the air with its forefeet. Frank tumbled backward out of the saddle and landed hard on his back . . . his rifle discharged harmlessly in the air and fell from his grasp. He grunted, momentarily too stunned to think, until he heard the clump of boots running toward him.

Clawing his pistol free, he fired at a moving shape until his Colt was empty, its hammer clicking on a spent cartridge. In a daze he saw Raymond fall flat on his face less than twenty yards from where he lay. His horse galloped off, the sound covering the cries of a wounded man near the doorway, and Frank knew it was Lefty's voice he heard.

"You're a dead man fer shootin' my brother!" Cotton Polk screamed as he ran out of the hut wielding his pistol.

He came racing at Frank like an enraged bull, his lips drawn back in a grimace.

Frank rolled to his left to make a grab for his rifle, all the while knowing he would be too late to lever a shell and aim and fire. His heart was thudding inside his chest . . . he felt sure he was about to die.

Off to the right, from a corner of the hut, a gun blasted. Cotton was lifted off his feet, tossing his pistol high above his head as he started to fall. He landed on his chest, skidding over loose caliche until he slid to a stop.

Frank shook his head, trembling, experiencing real fear for the first time in his life.

"I got him, Frank," Bob said, sounding almost calm about it. He walked away from the hut brandishing a smoking six-gun. "You was dead right, the way you had it figured. They came out here to backshoot Lefty. We got here just in time to save the money, but it looks like it's too late for Lefty."

"Son of a bitch," Frank snarled, climbing unsteadily to his feet. "Cotton woulda killed me if you hadn't come along when you did."

"I was waitin' to see what happened, Boss. Didn't think nothin' was wrong at first. I was fixin' to walk up when I heard Cotton shoot out the window."

"Let's see how bad Lefty's wound is," Frank said, holstering his empty revolver.

"It's mighty bad, Frank. Cotton shot him plumb between his shoulders the way a yellow son of a bitch kills a man, from the back side. Never would have guessed it . . . not from him or Raymond neither."

Frank walked over to Lefty. Blood was pouring from a hole in his back. "Damn," he whispered angrily. "We lost a good man tonight, a good man to ride the trails with."

Bob pointed his pistol at Raymond and Cotton. "I would have said the same 'bout them other two, till tonight."

Frank stared into Bob's eyes. "Always remember this . . .

when there's enough money involved, a man ain't got many friends he can count on.''

Bob nodded. ''It's a lesson, all right. I'll make damn sure both them Polk brothers is dead. If'n they ain't, I'll put a bullet in their goddamn brains for what they done to my friend Lefty.''

''Do it!'' Frank said, his senses returning after the hard fall off his horse.

Bob sauntered over to Raymond, bending down for a closer look in the darkness. ''He ain't dead yet,'' Bob said, cocking his pistol. The bang of a gun echoed across the desert. Raymond's body jerked when a fountain of blood squirted from a hole in the back of his skull. ''He is now,'' Bob added tonelessly. ''He had it comin' for what he done.''

Frank walked over to Lefty Sikes, recalling the years they'd ridden the outlaw trail together. He knelt down. Lefty moaned softly, but his eyes were closed. ''Sorry, ol' hoss,'' Frank said as he touched Lefty's shoulder. ''I reckon it's my fault. I should have left Bob out here with you to watch over the loot. I don't figure them Polks woulda tried anything against the two of you.''

Bob was standing beside Cotton with his gun aimed down. A humorless grin twisted his mouth. ''Look here, Frank. This sorry sumbitch is tryin' to crawl away. Maybe he still thinks he's gonna get his hands on our money.''

Frank drew his Colt, flipped open the loading gate, and began ejecting spent shells. ''Let the bastard suffer a while, Bob,'' he said. ''He's earned it. Maybe he's wishin' right now he'd stayed at the cantina , , ,''. A movement in the doorway of the hut almost made Frank jump out of his skin. The girl who rode out with Raymond stood in the door frame with her hand over her mouth, trying to stifle a scream while she stared at the bodies. ''Shut up, bitch!'' Frank warned, preparing to reload his pistol, pushing cartridges out of the loops on his gunbelt. ''Get back inside.'' He spoke to Bob over his shoulder. ''Bob, you an' me are gonna stay here the rest of the night. We'll fuck this girl long as we can, to pass some time. Right now, after what just happened, I don't trust nobody else but you an' me to watch over the money.''

"It *is* a helluva lot of money, Frank," Bob said, a change in his voice. "You're holdin' an empty gun, an' mine's still loaded an' ready."

Frank made a quarter turn toward Bob, staring at him across the hardpan between them as short hairs stirred on the back of his neck. A distance of only thirty or forty feet separated them. "What are you sayin'?" he asked. Down deep, he knew what Bob meant, what he meant to do. Bob's greed had gotten the best of him. He wanted all the money for himself.

"I could kill you right now an' all that money's mine," Bob said.

Frank knew he had to think fast. "The others . . . Wilson an' Clyde an' Josh an' Sonny. They'd come after you as sure as flies come to shit."

"It'd be mornin' before they knowed what's happened. I'd be miles from here by then."

"I had you figured for a man I could trust . . . *really* trust, like I did Lefty."

"You was the one who told me on the way out here a man ain't got many friends when it comes to a bunch of money. Remember what you said, Frank?" Bob slowly lifted the muzzle of his Colt until it was pointed at Frank. "Maybe there was some real wisdom in them words."

"They'd track you down, the others would. Wouldn't no place on earth be safe."

"Maybe."

"Ain't no maybe to it. Some night, when you was asleep, ol' Josh Walker might come slippin' through your window with that big bowie knife of his. He'd cut your throat an' you'd never wake up to spend the money you had left."

"That could happen, I reckon, only I'd be real careful about where I went to bed every night."

Frank had to buy more time. "Let's just you an' me take it, so there'd be one to watch the other's backside. We can load it on these horses an' clear out now."

"I couldn't trust you, Frank. Never did, not the way I trusted Lefty."

"You'll have to trust somebody. One man standin' alone ain't got a chance against four more hot on his trail. If Josh didn't get you, Sonny or somebody else will."

Bob was thinking, chewing his bottom lip. Then he grinned and lowered his Colt to his side. "Hell, Frank, I was just funnin' you. Let's you an' me do like you said . . . load the money an' clear out."

Frank took a deep breath. "You had me scared for a minute, Bob. But a man's gotta have a partner if he's in the outlaw trade. You an' me, we'll be partners. Go ahead an' finish off that double-crossin' Cotton Polk an' let's go inside an' get the money."

Bob nodded and gave a weak grin. "I'd have never done it, Frank. You got my word on it. Maybe I had too damn much tequila tonight, playin' a dumb joke on you like that."

"I never believed you'd go through with it," he said as Bob aimed for the back of Cotton Polk's head.

The explosion startled the horses tied in front of the hut and one broke its reins, trotting off toward the desert snorting through its muzzle. The Mexican girl let out a muffled cry with one hand covering her mouth.

These distractions were enough to allow Frank to slip three cartridges into the empty cylinder of his pistol, then twirl it and close the loading gate unnoticed.

Cotton groaned once more and lay still.

"He's a dead sumbitch now," Bob said, looking in Frank's direction.

Frank's Colt was aimed at Bob Walls. "And so are you, you double-crossin' bastard!" he snarled, pulling the trigger.

Bob folded up like a linen napkin with his hands covering a hole in his belly. His gun fell to the ground between his boots before he sank to his knees, gazing up at Frank with pain-shuttered eyes. "I . . . was . . . only funnin'," he gasped, toppling over on his face.

16

Comandante Valdez embraced Slocum, as was the Mexican custom among close friends. After a few hours of sleep and a delicious meal of spicy goat meat, beans, and tortillas, Slocum was ready for the sixty-mile ride to Piedras Negras. He and the *comandante* talked about border troubles, a building revolution in the south of Mexico, and many other things, including women.

"We have no telegraph," Valdez said while Slocum tightened the cinch on his Thoroughbred stud. "But if you find these men in Piedras Negras, have one of Capitan Vela's men bring word to me. I will see that they are punished, even though they have broken no laws in Mexico that I know of."

"I'll get word to you somehow," Slocum said, climbing into the saddle.

"I have the suspicion," Valdez added, "that these robbers are responsible for whatever has happened to Manuel Garza, the soldier who is still missing. If I could prove this, I can send the Americanos to prison."

"The main thing I'm after is getting the army's money back and ending these train robberies. If I can find that bunch, I aim to try."

"Do not trust Enrique Vela," Valdez warned. "I am sure

121

he is taking bribes from some Americano outlaws to keep them safe in his village. Do not trust him. It is most unfortunate that a *capitan* in *los federales* can be so dishonest, yet I fear it is true of him.''

''I'll keep that in mind, Porfirio. And thanks again for all the hospitality, and feeding my horse. I'll ride beside the river most of the way. Maybe I can find out what happened to your soldier.''

Valdez bowed politely and grinned. ''Good luck, amigo. Go with God, and never turn your back on Capitan Vela or his men. It is sad that I must warn you of this, but things in Mexico are not as they used to be.''

''I understand. One way or the other, I'll let you know what I find in Piedras Negras. *Adios,* my friend.''

He swung his horse around and struck a trot through the gate into the presidio, turning southeast to ride along the Rio Grande road. Slocum had a feeling, as he was leaving Villa Acuna and Comandante Valdez, that the peaceful part of his search for the stolen army payroll was about to end.

Riding beside the river, he passed a few slow-moving burro carts and an occasional *vaquero* until he struck open rangeland below the river. The few small farms he saw were impoverished, and as the land became drier, even the farmhouses were absent. Mile after mile of desert lay on both sides of the Rio Grande, and he found he was the only traveler on this road as dusk turned to darkness.

He was dressed in denims and a bib-front blue shirt, his better clothes tucked inside his bedroll. A short .32-caliber bellygun was hidden inside his shirt, and his bowie was sheathed in his right boot. In most cases this was his battle garb, unless an occasion arose when he had to fight without the time to prepare. But he was prepared now, for Frank Clanton and his gang and whatever else lay in store for him in the tiny Mexican village of Piedras Negras.

His bay stud trotted easily through the cooler hours of the night, taking him ever closer to his destination. He put his mind on the robberies, for there was still one important link to Frank Clanton's success that was missing. At the moment Slocum had no idea as to who was letting Clanton know which trains to rob, but he felt we was closer to finding out *how*. Comandante Valdez had said there was a telegraph line linking San Antonio to the Texas town of Eagle Pass, across the river from Piedras Negras. One of Clanton's men, or even Clanton himself, must have gone across to get the messages from San Antonio that told him when a train with an army payroll would pass through Devil's River Canyon. And each message had to come well in advance, giving Clanton enough time to ride up to the canyon from Piedras Negras and pull the spikes out of one rail, making it hard for the train crew to see at night that a derailment was about to happen.

"It'll all fall together," Slocum told himself, listening to the regular clump of his horse's hooves on dry roadbed. More than anything else, if he could he aimed to get the money back to the Texas and Pacific, for Malcom's sake.

An old Mexican driving a burro cart was moving down the road when Slocum rounded a bend at sunrise. The old man heard him and turned to look over his shoulder.

Slocum drew alongside the cart, slowing his horse. "How far to Piedras Negras?" he asked.

The driver shrugged as though he didn't understand English. Then he saw Slocum pointing southeast. The driver held up two fingers and said, *"Dos horas."*

Slocum nodded that he understood, and urged his stud past the cart, saying, *"Gracias."*

By pushing his horse he knew he could cut the time in half and with that in mind, he sent the bay to a short lope to cover as much ground as he could. For a quarter hour he held a steady gait, watching the road ahead. Time always seemed to pass too slowly when he was in a hurry.

Off in the distance he spotted a lone horseman coming toward him at a lope. It was unusual to find someone else moving along this road in a hurry. And the closer he came to the rider the more he sensed trouble. For reasons he could never explain, there were times when he could almost feel danger, like a breath of hot wind blowing gently across his cheeks.

He drew back on the reins and slowed his stud to a trot with his eyes glued on the approaching horseman. The cowboy wore a gray Stetson pulled low in front, and he wore a gunbelt. A rifle butt jutted from a boot tied to his saddle.

He's heavily armed, and in a hurry, Slocum thought, wondering if the rider might be one of Clanton's men. Some gangs cut up their robbery loot and went separate ways until things died down, not wanting to attract too much attention. As a form of insurance, Slocum took the hammer thong off his Colt and slowed his horse to a walk.

The oncoming stranger suddenly seemed apprehensive, for he too reined down to a walk, then a complete stop when he was a few dozen yards away. His right hand moved toward his gun, and that was all Slocum needed to return the gesture in kind.

Slocum's .44/.40 came out cat-quick, before the cowboy had his gun out of leather. "Don't do it!" Slocum shouted. "Don't pull that piece or I'll blow your arm off."

The man's jaw turned to granite. "You got no call to pull no gun on me, stranger."

"You were reaching for yours. Reason enough."

"Just bein' careful, is all."

"Same goes for me, only you reached first. Now put both hands on your saddlehorn till I find out who you are and why you'd reach for a gun when you set eyes on me."

"Are you some kinda law?" the rider asked, looking Slocum up and down. He slowly took his hand from the butt of his pistol and placed both palms atop his saddlehorn.

"Would it worry you if I told you I was?"

"I'd inform you that you ain't got no jurisdiction on this side of the Rio Grande." It was clear the stranger was afraid of something.

Slocum edged his horse closer, still pointing the muzzle

of his pistol at the stranger. "You seem mighty well informed on the laws here in Mexico. Makes a man wonder why, if you ain't broken any laws either place."

"I know what's legal an' what ain't."

Slocum stopped when he reached the man's side, his gun aimed at the cowboy's ribs. "You ever hear of a man named Frank Clanton?" Slocum asked.

The look of recognition Slocum expected crossed the cowboy's face. "You *are* the law, ain't you?" As he said it he made a lunge for Slocum's pistol, a move Slocum had anticipated well ahead of time.

Slocum drove his fist into the rider's chin. A cracking noise followed as the cowboy went cartwheeling off his horse to the ground, landing with a thump.

Slocum was down off his bay before the stunned man could lift his head. He bent down and placed the muzzle of his Colt between the cowboy's lips. "Listen to me real close, mister, 'cause I'm only gonna say this once. I'll kill you so quick you won't know what hit you. The last thing you're gonna see is the sky over your head. Are you paying attention?"

The cowboy's eyes flickered from Slocum's gun barrel to his face. He had some trouble answering with cold steel against his front teeth. "I'm listenin'."

"What's your name?"

"Devers. Clyde Devers."

"And you robbed that train in Devil's River Canyon with Frank Clanton, didn't you?"

Devers needed a moment to nod his head.

"Where's Clanton and the money?"

"Frank'll kill me if'n I tell."

"And I'm gonna kill you if you don't. Make no mistake about it, Mr. Devers. I work for the Texas and Pacific Railroad. I don't have to explain to anybody what happened to you. Comandante Valdez at Villa Acuna is a friend of mine, and all I'll have to do is tell him you drew on me first. Now where's Clanton, and where's the money?"

"I . . . got part of it in my saddlebags . . . my share. Came to nine hundred dollars."

Slocum did a little quick math. "That's more'n one share if there was nearly a dozen of you."

"Some of the boys got crossways the other night an' tried to steal all of it. They shot it out betwixt 'em, an' Frank showed up just in time. Ain't but five of us left, an' we decided to split up till things cooled off. Please don't kill me, mister. I done told you what you wanted to know."

"You didn't tell me where Clanton and the rest of the money is."

"They's still in Piedras Negras. I lit out soon as I got my share."

"That leaves four," Slocum said.

"That's right. Four, includin' Frank. They was gettin' drunk again last night, so I made up my mind to pull out fer a little place called Hidalgo this mornin', afore one of 'em got drunk an' decided to kill me for my share."

"Where are they staying in the village?"

"A little adobe south of town. Mostly, they hang around at the Agave Cantina. There's whores an' food an' plenty of tequila an' pulque."

"Get on your feet and hand over your share of the money. You do like I say and I won't kill you."

"You gonna put me in jail?"

"I sure am, only we're going across the river so I can lock you up on the Texas side in Eagle Pass. Now get up, before I change my mind and put a tunnel through your head."

Devers came slowly to his feet. Slocum jerked the man's pistol out and tossed it in the Rio Grande. "Get me the money, and if you sneeze wrong, you're dead."

"They'll hang me sure in Texas."

"I'll kill you just as surely if you don't go back peaceful as hell."

"I ain't lookin' to die."

"Maybe the judge will consider that you gave up without a fight. Might give you a shorter sentence."

Devers turned slowly toward his saddlebags as if he expected to be shot in the back. He opened one pouch and took out a sack with "Planters Bank" printed on it.

Slocum tucked the money inside his shirt. Walking to Devers's horse, he pulled the Winchester from its boot and said in a quiet voice, "Get back in the saddle. Ride in front of me. If anything goes wrong, I'm not gonna explain the loud noise you hear behind you. Hell, you won't be alive long enough to figure out what it was."

Devers obediently stepped in a stirrup and swung aboard his horse, waiting for Slocum to mount.

"Head back the way you came, Mr. Devers, and pray real hard my horse don't stumble so this gun goes off accidentally. I sure wouldn't want that to happen to a nice feller like you."

Devers reined his horse around and aimed for Piedras Negras, and the crossing over to Eagle Pass. Slocum was satisfied, for the moment. He'd learned a good many important things . . . where to look for Clanton and the others in Piedras Negras, and that some of the outlaws had already done him the favor of killing each other in a shootout over the money. And he knew he was only up against four outlaws now.

Lady Luck had delivered one of the train robbers right into his hands, and not a shot had been fired, although Slocum's knuckles hurt some from the blow he'd delivered to Devers's chinbone. All in all, things were headed in the right direction.

Half an hour later, after listening to one more plea from the outlaw to set him free, which Slocum declined with a wave of his gun, they rode into view of two small towns nestled across from each other on the banks of the river.

"We'll cross over right here," Slocum said. "No point in letting Mr. Clanton know I'm here . . . until I'm good and ready."

17

The sheriff in Eagle Pass introduced himself as Ben Wheeler, getting up from behind a battered wood desk tilted on one broken leg. Sheriff Wheeler saw the gun in Slocum's hand and declined to offer a handshake. Then he eyed Clyde Devers, sizing him up the way some men do a horse. Wheeler was close to sixty, with a sun-weathered face and snow-white hair. He carried an older-model Walker Colt high on his hip, as if he wasn't in the habit of using it much.

"John Slocum," Slocum said, introducing himself. "This is Clyde Devers, one of the train robbers who hit the Texas and Pacific line up in Devil's River Canyon. I carry a letter of legal authority to act for the railroad. I want this man locked up in that jail cell behind you until I can notify the Texas Rangers. After this thief is behind bars, you can direct me to the telegraph office."

"Right next to the post office, Mr. Slocum," Wheeler said, taking a key from his desk drawer. "I'll lock this teller up now, but I want a look at that letter you're carryin'. We get lots of bounty hunters down this way who ain't got no legal authority to spit."

Slocum ushered Devers into the cell, and waited until the key turned in the lock before he put his pistol away. "I'll get that letter from my saddlebags," he said. "And one more thing. You might want to know that an outlaw by the name of Frank Clanton is across the river in Piedras Negras. I spoke to Comandante Valdez in Villa Acuna, and he warned me that a Capitan Vela in charge of the post over there might be offering some bad characters a safe haven, even from bounty hunters or railroad investigators like me. But Clanton is there, and so are three others."

"I'd heard," Wheeler said, tossing the key on the desktop. "I know all about Cap'n Vela, but there ain't a damn thing I can do. He's in charge over yonder, an' he does pretty much whatever he pleases, unless one of his commanding officers shows up. He puts on a better act those times."

Slocum made to go outside for the letter. He paused at the door. "Do you recall any Americans like Devers ever coming across to the telegraph office? Maybe only once in a while, but they'd come from Piedras Negras, most likely."

Wheeler's shoulders slumped. "A few times. I had my own suspicions then . . . not 'bout no train robberies, but I figured they was men on the dodge from the law on this side. Look, Mr. Slocum, I'm an old man, sixty-three, an' this job don't pay much at all. I ain't no match for a sure-'nough shootist, so unless somebody breaks the law here in Eagle Pass, I mind my own business an' leave 'em alone. A man lives longer that way, an' he don't get holes shot through him."

"I understand, Sheriff. No need to explain. I'll get that letter, and then I've got to send a wire to Fort Worth to the main office of the railroad, to let them know I got some of their money back, and one prisoner. I'll also notify the Rangers to pick this gent up as quick as they can."

"What about them others? Clanton?"

"I'm going across after them, and the money. I'll wait till it gets dark. The place is too small and everyone in the village will see me ride the crossing. My chances will be better at night. My prisoner told me they hang out at the Agave Cantina.''

''Pedro's place. Pedro Villareal is a nice enough feller, but he needs to make money like everybody else. Runs a few whores an' sells some food mostly.''

''Frank's gonna kill you when you show up,'' Devers said from his jail cell, clinging to the bars with both hands, a lump on his jaw where Slocum had knocked him off his horse.

Slocum gave him a short grin. ''He's damn sure gonna get the chance to try, if he's fool enough.''

Slocum sent the following wire to Malcom Warren:

FOUND CLANTON IN PIEDRAS NEGRAS **STOP** CAPTURED ONE PRISONER AND SOME OF MONEY **STOP** GOING AF-TER CLANTON TONIGHT **STOP** WISH ME LUCK **STOP** SLOCUM **END**

He followed this message with a request that a Texas Ranger pick up Clyde Devers at the Eagle Pass jail, to be bound over for trial charged with robbery of the Texas and Pacific Railroad and more charges might follow. He signed the telegram, ''John Slocum, Special Agent, Texas and Pacific.''

The telegraph operator, a chubby Mexican with a bald spot on top of his head, read through the telegram to the Rangers' office in San Antonio aloud before he went to the telegraph key. When he was finished reading, Slocum nodded. ''That's what I want sent. How much do I owe you?''

''Fifty cents, Señor. Twenty-five cents for each one.''

''I've got one more question.'' Slocum continued, resting his elbows on the counter. ''Does an American come over from Piedras Negras once in a while to pick up a telegram? It might be for a feller named Frank, or maybe one of his friends.''

''This kind of information would be confidential, Señor.

I would be violating telegraph company rules to tell you this. I am sorry.''

Slocum took out the same letter he'd shown Sheriff Wheeler a few minutes ago. ''I'm a railroad investigator. Here's my letter of authorization from the Texas and Pacific Railroad. Makes me a peace officer with legal authority. If you want, I can have the sheriff walk over here to identify me, and that makes it legal for you to tell me what I need to know.''

The operator read Slocum's letter quickly, a frown wrinkling his face. He said nothing for a moment, glancing from Slocum to the letter.

''You want me to fetch the sheriff?'' Slocum asked.

The Mexican let out a sigh. ''No, Señor. That will not be necessary.''

''Then tell me who comes for the messages, and how he knows when they're here.''

''I only know him as Señor Frank. When a telegram comes for him, I send the little boy, Paco, over to Piedras Negras on his burro to inform this man he has a message. Someone comes, a tall man with blue eyes. He always carries a pistol. He pays me one extra dollar every time I send Paco across the river to tell him about his message, and he is very generous with Paco as well.''

''What do these messages say? And where do they come from?''

The man swallowed. ''They are different. I do not remember them well. They say something about meeting him on a certain day of the week. That part is very strange, because they do not say where. They come from our office in San Antonio. This is all I remember.''

Slocum was coming to the most important part, for now he had proof Clanton was getting his information from San Antone, just like he'd figured all along. ''Who signs them? Is it the same name every time?''

The operator grinned. ''It is a strange name, and yes, it is the same each time. They are sent by someone calling herself the Yellow Rose. Obviously, it is a woman.''

Slocum's guesswork had proved correct. Rose was the source of Clanton's information. When he got back to San Antonio, he still had to find out who was giving the information to her.

He took the letter from Malcom back and stuffed it into his pants pocket. ''You've been very helpful,'' he said, placing one silver dollar on the counter. ''This is for you.'' He put fifty cents more to one side. ''And this is for the two wires. I want them sent right away.''

''Of course, Señor.''

''One more thing,'' Slocum said, turning for the door. ''Tell me where I can buy a straw sombrero and a serape.''

''The boy, Paco, can show you. He is sleeping on a pallet in the shade behind the office. I will wake him up and you can send him across the river on his burro to buy these things for you, only I must confess, Señor, I am puzzled.''

Slocum grinned. ''No real reason. Just always did want to own them, for a keepsake. Don't get down this way much and they would look good hanging on my wall back home.''

It was almost ten o'clock that night when Slocum sent his horse into the river crossing, bound for Piedras Negras. He wore a straw sombrero that covered his features, and the serape fit over his shoulders, hiding his gunbelt. From a distance he might resemble a Mexican *vaquero* riding a good, perhaps even a stolen, horse into Mexico.

The boy, Paco, had been a good source of information about the village. A smaller cantina, El Caballero, sat closer to the river than the much larger Agave Cantina, and from there Slocum would have a view of the larger place. Paco said few people went to El Caballero at night since the Americano outlaws were in town. And Paco told Slocum what he knew about the shootings, what the big outlaw who called himself Frank had told everyone. Some of his men had gotten drunk and held a gunfight amongst themselves.

Four were dead, one had cleared out of town, and only four remained in Piedras Negras now. Capitan Vela had ordered his *soldados* to carry the dead bodies away. Things were more peaceful now, according to Paco, while Frank and the men with him spent more money on tequila and whores and the best food in the village.

Under the cover of darkness, poorly disguised as a *vaquero* in his straw hat and serape, Slocum headed for what he hoped would be his showdown with Frank Clanton and the last of his gang.

In the middle of the river he could hear faint guitar music coming from the Mexican side. Windows along the main road into the village glowed with lamplight, casting squares of pale yellow onto the caliche. No one seemed to notice him as he came closer to the riverbank. The few people who walked in front of stores and cantinas in Piedras Negras paid little attention to a man in a sombrero and serape making the crossing.

As soon as he rode out of the river he swung away from the middle of town, following Paco's instructions to an alley behind El Caballero where the boy had agreed to meet him tonight to keep an eye on his horse. Paco's eyes had almost popped from his skull when Slocum had given him two more silver dollars to watch the stud while he drank a few shots of tequila and enjoyed himself. This was what he'd told the boy, for it was all Paco needed to know about the reasons for Slocum's visit to Piedras Negras.

He found the alleyway and rode cautiously behind a small bakery, a *mercado* where fruits and vegetables were sold, then past the rear of a pottery shop, until he came to the back door of the cantina where Paco, straw sombrero in hand, waited for him in the shadows.

Slocum swung down and gave the boy the reins. "Might be a while," he said. "And if you hear any shooting from those bad hombres down the street, make sure you take my horse back over to Sheriff Wheeler's office in Eagle Pass."

"*Sí, Señor.* I will lead it across with my burro. You can

trust Paco. And you are a very generous man too.''

He clapped the boy on the shoulder and entered the cantina through its rear door, pausing long enough to make sure none of Clanton's men were inside. A lone Mexican cowboy sat at a table near a front window, sipping from a gourd dipper of pulque as he watched the street.

A pretty young girl behind the makeshift plank bar seemed surprised when Slocum came in from the rear, and even more surprised when she saw his face clearly.

''Why do you come in this way, Americano?'' she asked.

''Left my horse out back with a friend,'' he replied, handing her a silver coin. ''Bring me a shot of your best tequila. I came in the back on account of I'd heard there were some mean *pistoleros* in town.''

The girl palmed the coin quickly and smiled. Then her face turned serious as she took a bottle from a shelf behind the bar. ''It is true, Señor, about the *pistoleros*. Last night, some of them killed each other. Everyone in the pueblo could hear the shooting even though it was outside of town, on the road to Nava.''

''I heard about it over in Eagle Pass,'' Slocum said, taking a seat at another empty table near a window. He nodded to the old *vaquero* and continued talking to the woman. ''I sure as hell don't aim to get killed over a few drinks.''

She brought him a brimming shot glass full of clear liquid, and he knew how fiery it would be drinking it down.

''Why do you wear the sombrero and serape when you are not Mexicano?'' she asked, smiling a pretty smile full of pearly white teeth.

''Didn't particulary want to draw any attention to myself while I was here. Didn't want to get shot at. The gunmen are from Texas, I was told, and they'd be more likely to start some kind of trouble with another Americano.''

She waited by his table while he tasted his drink, and true to his prediction, the tequila was like liquid fire passing down his throat. He took a deep breath. ''What's your name?'' he asked her when his throat cooled some.

"Isabela," she replied, smoothing the front of her sack-cloth dress.

He glanced at her figure. Her breasts were small but firm enough to stand out from her chest. Her waist was thin, and her calves showing below the hem of her skirt were shapely. "I'd like to spend some time getting to know you, Isabela. My name's John . . . Juan in *Español*."

Her cheeks colored slightly. "We are not busy tonight," she told him, sitting down in a chair opposite his. "Ever since the *malo pistoleros* came to Piedras Negras, the villagers stay home at night. They are very afraid."

Slocum glanced down the street to the front of the Agave Cantina, hearing laughter and music coming from inside. "Maybe that'll end soon," he said quietly, without explaining how he intended to make things safe again for the people of Piedras Negras.

18

Wilson Giles stood at a window of the Agave watching the road, a bottle of tequila in his fist. Sonny Jones sat at a table behind him, sucking on the nipple of a young Mexican whore's breast. Josh Walker was in one of the back rooms with another whore. Frank had Carmen seated at a corner table, running his hand up her dress, playing with her cunt with his finger while a guitar strummed softly, played by a woman at the bar.

Carmen had tears glistening in her eyes from the pain Frank's finger caused when he stabbed it roughly into her mound.

"How come you're cryin' again, bitch?" he asked. "All you know how to do is cry, you lousy whore."

"You are hurting me," she whimpered, keeping her voice down low.

"I'm gonna hurt you real bad if you don't quit all the damn cryin'," he snapped, glaring at her, then tossing back a shot glass of tequila. He looked across the room at Wilson. "What the hell are you so goddamn busy lookin' at, Wilson? Ain't a damn thing out there to see 'cept more Mexicans. Looks like you'd have seen enough of them lately."

Wilson turned from the window, his hollow-cheeked face

devoid of expression. "I seen this big feller ridin' across the river a while ago, ridin' a damn good horse, only he turned off someplace. He ain't rode by here yet. Makes me wonder if it could be some bounty hunter."

"You're too damn jumpy," Frank said. "Besides, we got all sorts of protection from that Cap'n Vela if some son of a bitch shows up. He took our money to make damn sure nobody bothers us here."

"Just seemed unusual, that he didn't ride this way. Ain't but two roads through this shit-hole town."

Sonny spoke up. "You got that right, Wilson. This is a fuckin' shit-hole if I ever seen one. Wasn't fer this whore's pretty tits, I'd have cleared out when Clyde did."

"Nobody's stoppin' you from leavin' now," Frank said, as he shoved his finger hard and deep into Carmen's cunt again. "You can ride out any time you please. That goes for the both of you. Me an' Josh'll stay here an' fuck all these whores to death."

Wilson stared back out the window. "I reckon there's been enough dyin' in this town. Sure was bad, how Raymond an' Cotton tried to rob us. Never woulda guessed it."

"Real bad 'bout Lefty an' Bob gettin' themselves killed to save our money," Sonny said. "Good thing you come along when you did, Frank, in time to blow Cotton's head off 'fore he got away with everything."

Frank nodded, pouring himself another drink. "Too bad about all them boys. Like I told you, I didn't have no choice but to shoot Cotton when I seen what he was doin'. Raymond was already dead. So was Bob an' Lefty."

Wilson wouldn't let it go. "Never guessed Raymond an' Cotton woulda stole from us. We'd been together a while. I reckon money makes some men change . . . when it's enough."

"They got greedy," Frank said, adding to his story about the four dead bodies to make it sound as convincing as he could. "I never figured it about Cotton or Raymond neither. They was good men in a fight."

"So was Bob an' Lefty. Lefty saved me from gettin' my ass shot off durin' that second train robbery. One of them soldiers got around behind me, an' Lefty seen him. Lefty put a bullet plumb through him. I still feel like I owe him, even if he is dead now."

Sonny went back to sucking loudly on the girl's nipple, and she giggled, mussing his hair, pressing his face deeper into the fleshy mound of light brown skin.

"We all owed him," Frank said, playing his hand out all the way. "We owe Lefty an' Bob for layin' down their lives to save our loot till somebody got there. It was plain ol' good luck for me to show up right when I did."

Wilson continued to stare out at the dark. "Wish the hell I knew who that feller was an' where he went. Mighty goddamn odd that he never rode by."

"You worry too much, Wilson," Frank said. "It's gonna give you the bellyache. Why don't you take that gal playin' the guitar an' fuck her real hard. It'll take your mind off that feller you saw. Cap'n Vela's got men watchin' the river an' both roads into Piedras Negras. Ain't nobody gonna slip up on us without us knowin' it."

Wilson appeared to stiffen, his right hand falling near his holstered pistol. "Here comes one of Vela's soldiers now, an' he sure is walkin' fast. Maybe he seen that feller too. I got this feelin' somethin's wrong, Frank."

Frank took his finger out of Carmen, just in case he needed to reach for his Colt. He tossed back his fresh drink and got up from the table to walk over to the other window.

A uniformed *federale* carrying a rifle was hurrying toward the front of the Agave, glancing over his shoulder as he came.

"He does act a bit edgy," Frank agreed, wondering what could be bringing one of Vela's men to the cantina at such a rapid walk.

Sonny stopped sucking on the girl's teat to look at Frank and Wilson. "You reckon we got troubles?" he asked, pushing the girl off his lap.

"Can't say till he gets here," Frank replied.

The soldier seemed to be looking at the front of the little cantina named El Caballero as he hurried past it. It was a place Frank had never visited after he'd found out it didn't have any whores or food to offer.

"Walkin' real fast. Too fast," Wilson added.

Frank shook his head to clear it of the fog from too many glasses of tequila. If trouble *was* coming, he'd be as ready for it as he had been when three of his men had tried to double-cross him, and this time he wouldn't be caught with an empty pistol.

The young Mexican soldier entered the cantina, resting the stock of his carbine on the dirt floor. The girl playing the guitar stopped when she saw him come in. He looked around the room until he found Frank. "Señor Clanton, *por favor,* my English is no too good. This man come to tell Capitan Vela there be one gringo in jail across the river. This gringo be one man who is come here with you."

"In jail?" Frank asked, blinking once, unable to believe his ears. "How the hell did Clyde—it *has* to be Clyde— how did he wind up in jail?"

"Another gringo bring him, Señor. He have his gun stick in his back."

"Another gringo?" Frank's mind was racing.

Wilson spoke up. "I told you I seen this big feller ride over, only he never rode past this place. Could mean he's here now, watchin' us. Probably some goddamn bounty hunter hired by the railroad."

"Shit!" Frank hissed, turning to Sonny. "Go get Josh out of that whore's room. Tell him we got big troubles . . . that Clyde's over yonder in jail."

Sonny hurried through the back door. Frank addressed the *federale.* "Go tell your captain I want all his men out lookin' for this other gringo, if he's on this side of the border, the bastard who hauled Clyde to jail in Eagle Pass. Run tell Cap'n Vela what I said. I've paid him good money an' now I want somethin' for it. Tell him one of my men saw a stranger ridin' across the river a while ago.''

"He was wearin' a sombrero an' a serape," Wilson added, "but he was ridin' a mighty damn good horse to be a common *vaquero* in this part of Mexico.''

"Tell Cap'n Vela," Frank said again, "an' don't waste no damn time doin' it.''

"Si, señor,'' the soldier replied, turning on his heel to run out the door, boots thumping down the street until the sound began to fade.

"Get our rifles, Wilson,'' Frank said, searching the street himself, looking both ways without sticking his head out the opening. "We'll turn the tables on this goddamn man-hunter. We got him bad outnumbered, along with Cap'n Vela's men. We'll search every inch of this lousy town till we find him. Get them rifles, an' plenty of extra shells out of our saddlebags.''

Wilson backed away from the window and went out the back where their horses were tied. Frank kept an eye on the street, one hand resting on his holstered gun.

"Bring me that bottle of tequila, bitch!'' he said over his shoulder to Carmen.

Carmen quietly brought the bottle over and handed it to him, then slipped away. He pulled the cork with his teeth and took a swallow, wondering if a bounty hunter had truly come over the river after them. "He's gotta have guts,'' he said to himself while his gaze roamed up and down the empty road. One man, or so the soldier said, had captured Clyde Devers and taken him to jail in Eagle Pass. One man would have to be crazy to go up against a gang the size of his, even with their numbers severely reduced, a fact the bounty hunter wouldn't know about because the shooting had taken place last night here in Piedras Negras . . . unless this same manhunter had been watching them from hiding the whole time, waiting for the chance to take Frank and his boys one or two at a time, the way he'd done with Clyde.

He pondered how the bounty hunter could have followed

their trail to Piedras Negras. They'd been so careful to ride in the river's shallows for several miles, coming out on a stretch of rock where hoofprints would be hard to detect, except for the very best of trackers.

Then Frank began to wonder if Rose had double-crossed him by giving the details of their robbery plans and their hiding place to the law. "Rotten bitch," he whispered, thinking about her and how seductively beautiful she was. If she'd turned him in to the law or the railroad, she'd be in this up to her pretty little neck, he thought. "She'll go to prison . . . unless she cut a deal with one of 'em to save her own hide."

Wilson and Sonny came through the back with rifles and boxes of shells. Wilson strode over to the other window, levering a cartridge into the firing chamber of his Winchester.

"Josh said he'll be right here," Sonny said, coming over to stand beside Frank. "He said he was fixin' to bust his nuts in the whore an' he'd done paid his money. He don't act worried we got some bounty hunter after us. Josh said soon as he got his balls off in the whore, he'd go lookin' for whoever it is crossed the river."

Frank was mildly irritated, although he knew Josh Walker was a dangerous man when stalking a victim. He'd killed that soldier south of Villa Acuna with a throw of his knife, which few men could accomplish, and when it came to a duel with guns he was every bit as deadly.

"Wish them soldiers of Vela's would hurry up," Wilson said from his perch beside the window frame.

"Piss on them Mexican soldiers," Frank said. "They couldn't find their asses with both hands anyway. It'll be up to us to find this bounty man, whoever the sumbitch is. All them Mexican soldiers are gonna do is help us flush him out, wherever he's hidin'."

Sonny nodded his agreement. "I never seen a Meskin soldier who could shoot straight, or one who had a lick of sense. Seems like they look fer the dumbest Meskins they can find to put in their army.''

"You got that right,'' Wilson said, "an' them ol' rifles they carry are single-shot. Takes a Meskin soldier half an hour to figure out how to reload one.''

Frank wasn't paying much attention, his eyes locked on the street in front of the Agave. What Sonny and Wilson said was true, however. Most *federale* regulars were simple farmers who'd enlisted for the money. Few were given any training as soldiers, and the weapons they carried were out of date . . . old cap-and-ball pistols, early-model breech-loading rifles. But Vela's soldiers would force the bounty hunter out of hiding as they combed Piedras Negras, and that was the opportunity Frank was waiting for.

Josh came through the back door with his rifle. He spoke to Frank on his way over to a window. "Tell me what happened, Boss. Sonny said Clyde got put in jail over in Texas.''

"From what one of Vela's soldiers told us, one man captured Clyde an' locked him up across the river. Then Wilson claims he saw this big feller ridin' a good horse come across a while ago, only he didn't ride down this road. We figure it's the same gent who got Clyde, an' now the damn fool has come lookin' for us tonight.''

"He just made his first mistake," Josh promised, his close-set eyes flickering back and forth across buildings lining the road through town. "I'll slip out the back an' go find him for us. You boys stay here. I'll cut the bastard's throat an' bring you his goddamn scalp, the way an Injun does. Just make damn sure don't none of you shoot at me whilst I'm movin' around in town lookin' for him.''

"We'll be watchin'," Frank said. "Go find the son of a bitch an' kill him. He's either brave as hell, or the dumbest bastard on earth to come after us by himself.''

"Don't matter either way," Josh said as he wheeled for the back door. "Either way, he's gonna be dead.''

19

Slocum watched Isabela suck on a slice of lime, wishing it could be the head of his cock in her mouth now instead of a piece of fruit. "You have beautiful eyes," he told her, being careful what he said because the old *vaquero* on the other side of the room was surely listening, sipping slowly on his gourd dipper of pulque, pretending to be interested in what was going on outside when there was nothing to look at but an empty roadway.

"Thank you, Señor," she said, licking lime juice off her luscious full lips. Then she smiled. "What make you to come to Mexico?"

"I'm looking for a man. Several men, in fact. It's what I'd call a business trip."

"Why you look for these mens?"

"They owe me some money," he told her, which was only part of the truth.

"The mens no be here now," she said. "Everyone go away when *los pistoleros* come."

Slocum was distracted when he saw a soldier walking quickly down the street. The *federale* hurried past El Caballero and went to the front of the Agave. "Wonder what that's all about?" he asked himself aloud.

The old *vaquero* got up and placed a coin on the table.

He spoke to Isabela. *"Muchas gracias, Señorita."* He walked to the door and disappeared outside.

Isabela seemed worried about the old man's sudden departure, a slight frown wrinkling her brow. Slocum guessed the *vaquero* had been alerted by the soldier's sudden appearance, and that the soldier had gone inside the Agave, where Clanton and his men were headquartered.

"Something is bad now," Isabela said. "Bolivar would no go so quick if nothing is wrong."

"A soldier just went inside the Agave," Slocum said, "and he was in something of a hurry. . . ." He stopped talking when he saw the soldier come back outside and take off in the direction from which he'd come in a lumbering run. "Looks like Bolivar was right to leave when he did," Slocum added, coming out of his chair just as the *federale* ran past the window. "That soldier just brought those gunmen at the Agave some news, looks like, and they sent him back running."

"Is more trouble?" the girl asked, coming over to Slocum as he stood next to the window frame, holding his sombrero behind his back to keep from being noticed by anyone watching from inside the Agave.

"Maybe," he replied, staring into her chocolate eyes. "It might be a good idea if you closed down for the night, just in case."

"My father say I must stay open until midnight, Señor," she said.

"Your father doesn't know things could start happening here any minute. Close the doors and lock 'em, then go home by the back alley. I've got a feeling there's gonna be some shooting."

"Los pistoleros?" she asked, backing away from Slocum and the window.

"That's my guess. I'll go out the back way with you, to make sure you're safe after you lock up."

Isabela hurried to pinch out candles on two walls. Then she extinguished an oil lamp on each end of the bar, and suddenly the room was plunged into darkness, the only light coming from the street. She shuttered the windows from inside and slid iron rods into place. Then she locked a pair of creaking wooden doors with a bolt.

Slocum sauntered over to the rear door, opening it very carefully. Paco was standing outside holding Slocum's stud and his own burro. "Take my horse back across the river, Paco," he said softly. "There's gonna be some trouble, looks like. And be real careful crossing over."

"*Sí, Señor*. I will put your *caballo* in Sheriff Wheeler's barn and hang your saddle on a rail inside. I will be waiting there for you. *Buenas suerte*. Good luck, Señor."

The boy swung up on his donkey and led the stud down the alley. Slocum was about to put on his sombrero when he felt Isabela touch his arm.

"Thank you, Juan," she said. "*Gracias* for staying with me to close my father's place. You have a kind heart, not like *los pistoleros alla*."

"I'll walk you home, just to make sure you get there safe," he told her.

"I be safe. My father no understand why you come. No is need for you to go with me."

He grinned down at her. "May not be any need, but I'd like to anyway."

He saw her smile in light from the stars and moon shining down on the alley. Then she stood on her tiptoes and kissed him lightly on the lips. "You are *muy guapo*. I think in English it is word for handsome."

He bent down and returned her kiss. Then all at once he was alarmed by the sounds of Paco's burro and his horse coming back up the alleyway at a trot.

"Señor, Señor!" the boy cried softly. "Many soldiers are coming this way. Maybe they be looking for you."

Isabela locked a padlock on the back door of the cantina and turned quickly to Slocum. "I know place where you hide," she said. "Come." She took him by the arm and led him the other direction, away from the river, with Paco and the animals close behind.

"I'm only gonna make sure you and the boy are safe, Isabela," he whispered. "Then I'm going on my own. I've got that business to take care of I told you about."

Isabela froze in her tracks, staring at him. "You have business with *los malo hombres*?" she asked.

"I reckon so. I didn't want to tell you right off, but I have a score to settle with Frank Clanton and his men. It has to do with a train robbery. I work for a railroad that got robbed up in Texas."

"Dios!" the girl exclaimed, as the sounds of footsteps came from the far end of the alley. "Hurry, Juan. Follow me. I know a place where they no find you."

"It's you and the boy I'm worried about, and I don't aim to lose my horse. Show me where this place is, but let's get it done quick."

She turned, leading him between two dark adobe buildings to a back street of the village. Somewhere in another part of town a dog started to bark.

With his horse hidden in a slant-roofed shed, Slocum spoke to Paco. "You ride back across, son. There's sure to be some shooting and I don't want you hurt. They won't bother you if you hurry, before any trouble starts. Wake Sheriff Wheeler up and tell him what's going on, that I've found the rest of the train robbers and there's gonna be some gunfire on this side of the river tonight."

"But I would gladly stay, Señor."

"I appreciate it, but I want you out of here. Now go, or it'll be too late."

Paco's face was downcast as he swung up on his brown burro. He rode off at a shuffling trot, whipping his donkey with the ends of his reins.

Slocum turned to Isabela. "Now you go inside and stay there no matter what happens, no matter what you hear, and stay away from any windows."

She searched his face in the starlight. "You will kill them, Juan, is this true? Or maybeso they kill you."

He grinned, to reassure her "I'm a pretty hard man to kill, Isabela. Men have tried it before and didn't get the job done. Don't worry."

"But I do worry," she whispered, standing on her toes again to kiss him, this time allowing her lips to linger on his mouth while he put his arms around her.

She lingered in his embrace, until he heard a distant voice cry out, "Hey you, kid! Stop that goddamn donkey!"

Slocum whirled from the shed and took off in a run toward the voice, clawing his pistol free, tossing the sombrero away as he ran. There was no longer any need to pretend he belonged in this sleepy Mexican village, a village that was on the brink of awakening to the thunder of gunshots.

"You seen this big feller riding a bay horse?" the man who'd halted Paco demanded to know. "He rode across from Texas just a while ago. I know damn well you musta seen him. If you don't tell me the truth, I'm gonna cut your fuckin' throat."

Racing soundlessly on the balls of his feet, Slocum dodged back and forth between darkened huts until he came to a roadway where a cowboy, half hidden by dark shadows from a nearby store at a street corner, held Paco by the front of his shirt. A knife blade gleamed with starlight in the cowboy's hand as he held it near the bottom of Paco's chin.

"I don't see no big hombre ride a bay horse," Paco stammered as he was almost lifted off his feet, his sombrero falling off his head to the caliche road. "I don't see nobody, Señor. I swear it!"

"You lyin' little bastard! Tell me which way he went an' where he is now."

Slocum moved into the deepest shadows below the rooftop of the market, slowing to a walk, reaching into his boot. If this outlaw wanted to play with knives, it suited Slocum just fine. He understood the weapon as well as any he carried.

"One more time, you little Meskin bastard. Where did he go?"

Paco's eyes flickered toward Slocum's shadow as he was creeping up behind the outlaw, who was holding the knife to the boy's throat. "I swear I see no one, Señor!"

A fleeting second before Slocum was behind him, the robber glanced over his shoulder. He found himself staring Slocum in the face.

Slocum's left hand shot out to seize the wrist holding the bowie to Paco's neck, and when his fingers closed in an iron grip so the boy wouldn't be hurt, Slocum touched the tip of his own bowie to the cowboy's right side.

"So," Slocum hissed, "you like steel blades?"

As the words left his mouth he drove ten inches of razor-sharp iron into the outlaw's kidney and liver, ripping it up to his rib cage while he shoved it all the way to the hilt. Blood squirted over Slocum's right wrist and arm, and there was a soft snapping sound made by torn cartilage.

"Jesus . . ." the robber cried as his knees suddenly gave way. He let the knife fall from his hand. Then Slocum spun him around with his blade still buried deep in the man's belly.

"You like pickin' on kids?" Slocum snarled, his rage beyond control for an instant. "How does it feel to have your goddamn yellow guts cut out, asshole? You like sharp things? How does it feel to be on the other end, you dumb son of a bitch?"

The outlaw dropped to his knees, his lips moving rapidly, but no words came out.

"Die slow, you miserable bastard," Slocum said, jerking his bowie free.

"*Dios,*" Paco whispered, stepping back with his hands to his throat.

"Are you okay?" Slocum asked softly.

"*Sí, Señor.*"

"Then hop back on your jackass and get the hell across that river."

"You kill him," Paco gasped, reaching for the reins on his burro. "You kill him *pronto*."

"I'm gonna have to kill a few more," Slocum remarked, wiping the blood off his blade as the dying train robber toppled over on his back, blood pouring from a gaping gash across his side and his belly. "Now get moving. Don't stop for anything till you're on the other side."

Paco swung aboard his burro and drummed his heels into the animal's sides, riding to the street corner, where he turned to make for the Rio Grande.

Slocum took a final look at the man he'd cut, noticing his eyes had already begun to glaze over with death. "You had it comin', mister, whoever the hell you are. And so does Frank Clanton and the rest of his bunch."

The dying man's eyes wandered to Slocum's face. "Who . . . the hell . . . are you?" he croaked.

"Not that it makes any difference, pardner, but my name is John Slocum. Tell you straight, I don't give a damn what name you go by, 'cause you're a dead man now and nobody remembers the dead for long." He saw a bulge under the outlaw's shirt and bent down to see what it was. A bundle of bank notes taken from the train robbery was tucked under his belt and Slocum took it, a fairly large fistful of cash.

He heard footsteps, and caught a glimpse of two foot soldiers crossing a side street at a run. Both men were carrying rifles.

I've got no quarrel with them, he thought, turning the other way to make his approach toward the Agave Cantina. The *federales* were only following orders . . . he wouldn't harm any of them if he could help it.

Moving quickly from one dark shadow to the next, he began his assault on Frank Clanton's roost. If the prisoner he'd captured was telling the truth, only Clanton and two more of his men remained to be dealt with.

20

"Josh'll find him," Sonny said, leaning against a wood frame around the rear door into the Agave, keeping watch over their horses and for anyone approaching from the back alley. "When he does, we ain't got no more bounty hunter to worry about. Josh is a mean bastard when he's on the prod. I seen him cut a sumbitch nearly plumb in half one time up in Waco."

Frank was watching the street from a front window, standing off to one side holding his rifle. "Josh is plenty tough," he agreed, his mind on the stranger who rode into town. One man was the part that bothered him, why just one man had trailed them this far. There *had* to be others somewhere. Nobody would come after them alone. The stranger, whoever he was, must have wired for help as soon as he'd located Clyde and hauled him to jail in Eagle Pass. More bounty hunters would be on the way to smoke them out of hiding in Piedras Negras. It was time to clear out of this town and move deeper into Mexico, he decided, as soon as this fool who'd come across the river tonight was taken care of by Josh or the soldiers.

Wilson stood guard at the other window, keeping an eye on the movements of Captain Vela's soldiers passing back and forth on side roads through the village, rifles at the ready. "Josh moves real quiet," he said. "He told me he learned it from a Kiowa Injun scout a few years back, some redskin who scouted for the cavalry. Said it mattered how you put your foot down, some way or 'nother."

Frank saw a slender Mexican boy on a donkey riding fast in the direction of the river. He thought nothing of it, for most of the townspeople in Piedras Negras acted scared of him and his men, avoiding them on the streets whenever possible. The kid must have noticed the soldiers scouring the village and guessed something bad was about to happen.

Frank drained the last of the tequila from a bottle he'd carried to the window, and tossed it outside, shattering it in front of the cantina. "Bring me another bottle," he said to Carmen without turning around. "An' don't take all goddamn day doin' it."

"Sí, Señor," the girl said softly, hurrying over to the bar where a nervous bartender handed her a fresh bottle. She brought it over to Frank and pulled the cork before she gave it to him.

He took a deep drink, sleeving off his lips. "I been doin' some thinkin', boys. If this son of a bitch is a bounty hunter like we figure, he's already wired someplace for help. Means we got more gunmen headed our way. It's time we pulled out of this town."

"I've been thinkin' the same thing," Wilson said. "We got our horses saddled out back. Not a damn thing keepin' us here besides these whores an' a soft bed. I say we ride south soon as Josh gets back. Maybe head down to Nava or Aguas Calientes for a spell."

"We got enough money to go wherever the hell we please," Sonny said. "You know that railroad is offerin' a big reward fer us. It'll draw all sorts of hired guns, once word gets out where we're at. Clyde probably spilled his guts to the law over yonder, an' like you said, Frank, this damn bounty hunter who's after us now likely sent telegrams to some of his pardners, offerin' 'em a split if they lend him a hand bringin' us back, dead or alive. We got that Meskin cap'n in our pockets, but he won't be enough help if half-a-dozen paid shooters show up.''

"I still can't figure how he tracked us here," Frank said. "He must be mighty damn good at readin' sign. Maybe he's part Injun himself."

"He's gonna be all the way dead, soon as Josh finds him," Sonny declared. "Josh is a mean bastard with a knife or a gun."

Wilson drank from his own bottle of tequila. A silence filled the cantina until he spoke. "Josh sure is takin' his own sweet time about it. Hell, he's been gone maybe half an hour or more."

"That's 'cause he's real careful," Sonny said.

Frank was also beginning to wonder what was keeping Josh, why it was taking him and the soldiers so long to find a stranger in a village this small, only a couple of hundred people living here, eight or nine stores and two cantinas, maybe three-dozen adobe houses and smaller huts. "Could be the son of a bitch ain't here at all," Frank said.

Another silence passed. To Frank, it seemed the town was too quiet tonight. "Hell, that dog ain't even barkin' no more," he muttered, swallowing more tequila, waiting.

A soldier came running up the road, cradling his carbine to his chest. He ran up to the front door and stopped just inside, trying to catch his breath. "Señor Clanton! One of you men, he is dead! We find him just now. . . ."

"Dead?" Frank uttered the word in a hoarse whisper.

"*Sí, Señor*. He be cut open. *Mucho* blood, big hole here." The young *federale* pointed to his stomach.

"Damn," Wilson growled. "He got to Josh. . . ."

"Ain't possible," Sonny said, although his voice lacked conviction. "Nobody coulda slipped up on Josh with a knife an' killed him."

"Did anybody see the bastard?" Frank asked.

"No, Señor. We see nothing. Nobody."

"It can't be," Sonny insisted, softer than before.

Frank's mind was racing. Who could be good enough to kill a cautious man with experience like Josh Walker? he wondered. He had to be damn good, whoever he was. Then Frank remembered the money Josh was carrying. "Let's all three of us walk over to where they found the body so we can cover each other. Josh had some . . . valuables on him. Can't just leave it layin' there for somebody else to find."

"His share," Sonny said, as if it just dawned on him what Frank was talking about. "Unless the fella who killed Josh went an' found it already."

"We've gotta look," Frank said.

"We'll be out in the open," Wilson warned. "If this gent is any good with a rifle, he could cut us down from any one of them rooftops yonder. I don't like the idea. It's too damn risky."

"You want us to leave that money?" Frank asked, angry over Wilson's objections.

Wilson shrugged. "Can't spend it from a grave, Frank. I say we clear outta this shit-hole now. I've got this bad feelin' about who this bastard is. He ain't no tinhorn or he couldn't have snuck up on Josh without firin' a single shot. An' Clyde wouldn't have given up without no fight either. Maybe it's some honest-to-goodness bad son of a bitch, like Odell Pickett or Tom Spoon, on account of there's a big reward."

Frank hadn't given the bounty hunter's identity quite so much thought. "Tom Spoon was in prison, last I heard, an' Odell Pickett would have to come all the way down from Hell's Half Acre in Fort Worth. Besides, neither one of them would come after us by their lonesome."

"I can't believe he got ol' Josh," Sonny said, edgier than ever.

Frank spoke to the soldier. "Take us to where you found the body. We gotta look in his pockets." He turned to Sonny and Wilson. "C'mon, boys, an' keep them rifles up.

We'll walk down to where Josh's at, get his share, an' then ride south.''

"One of us oughta stay an' keep an eye on our horses so he don't put us afoot, Frank," Wilson said. "If he gets hold of our horses, we're stuck here."

Frank knew Wilson was worried, although he didn't show it the way Sonny did. "Okay, Wilson. You stand at the back door an' keep your gun coverin' our mounts. Me an' Sonny will go empty out Josh's pockets."

The *federale* turned on his heel and went to the doorway, looking out before he took another step, making sure the road was empty. Sonny trudged over to walk out behind Frank with his Winchester cocked and ready.

"This way," the soldier said, leading them toward the river while staying close to the fronts of stores where thatched-grass eaves and porches provided the darkest night shadows.

Frank followed the *federale*. Sonny brought up the rear. A few steps at a time, they advanced along the business district of Piedras Negras, to a little bakery standing on a street corner.

"There," the soldier said, pointing down the side road to a dark lump lying in the caliche.

Frank checked every rooftop before he said softly, "Let's go, Sonny, an' keep your eyes peeled. Shoot at anything that moves."

"Don't worry 'bout me bein' slow to shoot," Sonny remarked, edging along in Frank's wake as they crossed the street.

Frank let out the breath he was holding when they made it across. He approached Josh's corpse without really looking at it, expecting to hear a voice, or a gunshot, coming from some other direction.

He reached the body and bent down, forced to notice the huge gash opening Josh's belly, and the blood pooled around his still form. Frank searched every pocket and the waist of Josh's pants, getting blood on his hand. "It's gone.

Somebody beat us to it," he whispered, furious, for the risk of being shot at or dying had been taken for nothing.

"It had to be that bounty hunter," Sonny whispered back. "I hope he took it an' rode back across the river. Maybe now he's satisfied."

Frank remained doubtful. There was something eerie about the way this manhunter went about his business. "He's a sneaky son of a bitch. Let's get back to the cantina an' tell Wilson what happened. I reckon he was right. We oughta clear out of this town now."

"Suits the hell outa me," Sonny said, staring down at his dead friend. "Any son of a bitch who's good enough to kill Josh like that ain't nobody I care to tangle with."

"Maybe he just got lucky," Frank said, starting back to the corner, wiping Josh's blood off his palm and fingers before he gripped his rifle with both hands.

Suddenly a figure appeared between two adobes, and before Frank could think or see the man clearly, the outlaw brought his rifle to his shoulder and fired.

"Ayiii!" a shrieking voice cried. A *federale* soldier fell to the ground clutching his chest.

"Goddamn, Frank!" Sonny said. "You went an' shot one of Cap'n Vela's men."

The young soldier who'd escorted them to Josh's body dropped his rifle and put his hands to his face. *"Madre de Dios!"* he gasped. "It is Luis. . . ." He took off running toward his downed companion without regard for anything else.

Frank lowered his smoking Winchester, disgusted and angry with himself for being so damn jumpy. "We gotta clear out of this place now. I'll give Cap'n Vela some extra money so's he won't toss us in his jail."

"He could jail us anyhow, Boss, an' then he'd have all our money," Sonny warned.

Sonny was right. Things had quickly taken a badturn. Now they were wanted men on both sides of the Rio Grande. "Let's just get the hell outa here fast," he said, taking off in a run toward the cantina, still careful to stay close to buildings to keep from making a target of himself.

Wilson stiffened when he heard the gunshot. He turned away from the back door a moment to listen to an injured man's cries. Something had gone wrong, as he'd known it would. He'd told Frank he had a bad feeling about things now.

But as Wilson was listening to sounds from the road, a soft voice spoke to him from the darkness behind the Agave.

"Put down the rifle. Do it slow. I'm gonna kill you if you don't do just like I say. I already cut your pardner into chunks of fish bait. I've got a .44/.40 aimed at you now."

Wilson froze, eyes flickering across the inky space behind the cantina. His palms grew wet gripping his rifle stock. "You got the wrong man," he said, trying for a bluff. "I ain't with them boys. Just watchin' their horses, is all."

"This is the last time I tell you. Drop the rifle and get your hands real high in the air."

The voice came from a shadow beneath a small shed across the alley. Wilson decided to make his play.

He swung his rifle barrel toward the shadow and pulled the trigger. His heavy .44 banged, slamming into his shoulder, rocking him back on his boot heels.

A second explosion came from another spot just to the left of the shed, and Wilson felt something strike his breastbone with the power of a mule's kick. He was driven back, staggering, trying to keep his feet under him.

"Son of a . . ." Wilson felt himself falling. His head hit the floor and his vision blurred.

The thumping of boots running came nearer, and yet they still seemed so far away. He knew he'd been shot. His chest was on fire and he couldn't breathe. He thought about the money hidden in his boot, and that he might not live to spend it if his wound was serious. He heard one of the Mexican girls screaming.

Half in a daze, stunned, he felt someone's hands moving over him, and then his right boot was jerked off, the place where he kept the money. All he could see was a fuzzy shape standing over him. He couldn't make out the man's face.

A distant voice cried, "Wilson! Who's doin' the shootin'? Was that you?" It was Frank's voice, only Wilson couldn't hear it well because the damn whores were making so much noise, all the crying and shrieking.

Wilson drifted off to sleep, wishing he had known who had done the shooting when a bullet had been fired at him.

21

Slocum swung back behind the cantina doorway just as two men with rifles rushed up to the front door. A direct confrontation, a shootout, would be too chancy and he had no cover from a rear approach if the men split up. He decided to pull back to the shed and continue to play cat and mouse, until the right moment came to take one or both of the men into custody, or take them down. Without a description of Frank Clanton, he had no idea if he'd already killed the leader of the gang, and only time and happenstance would tell him if Clanton was still alive. But time was against him now, for the gunshots would draw Vela's soldiers to the cantina, worsening the odds he faced. Working alone, he had no choice but to continue moving to keep from being trapped.

He rushed to the side of the goat shed across the alley and pulled back out of sight. Voices came from the cantina, and he could hear them clearly enough to make out what was being said, although it was hard to hear because three young Mexican women inside were sobbing. The girls hadn't gotten a good look at him because they'd cowered behind the bar, which might prevent them from giving the last two members of the gang a good description of him.

"Shit! The bastard killed Wilson!" an angry voice declared when the thump of running boots stopped.

"He's gotta be out back somewhere, Frank. He's stealin' our horses right now, most likely. We'll be afoot, an' now them damn *federales* will be after us."

Now Slocum knew Frank Clanton was still alive. Four horses were tied to a stunted live oak tree just south of the cantina, with gear and saddlebags tied behind their saddles. The remark about Vela's men being after the outlaws was puzzling, hard to figure. Comandante Valdez had warned Slocum that Capitan Vela might be offering Clanton and his men protection, for the right amount of money.

"Means we gotta rush that back door, or go round to the back from both sides. Be careful, Sonny, but don't let the son of a bitch get to our horses. Cover me while I walk over an' see if the bastard got Wilson's share."

"I can already see he did, Frank. Wilson's right boot is off an' that's where he stashed his cut. Damn! This son of a bitch is robbin' us blind, an' killin' us off one at a time. I say we stick together an' move round back to our horses, so we can cover each other. Let's clear out now, afore he gets both of us."

A silence. Slocum cocked an ear to listen closely for the scrape of a foot, or the soft crunch of boots crossing hardpan. Few men knew how to move without making noise. It was a talent requiring practice, and a good teacher.

"We ain't gonna let nobody push us around," Frank's voice growled. "I ain't built that way, to take no pushin'. Stop the goddamn cryin', Carmen, an' tell me if you saw the bastard who shot Wilson. What did he look like?"

A woman's voice whimpered, "He was very big, Señor. He come so quick I no see him good. He look for money and then he go out the back door. I hide behind the bar with Consuela and Pedro so he don't shoot me."

"Did you get a look at him, Pedro?"

"No, Señor. I hide also. I no want to die."

"This ain't no ordinary feller, Frank. We ain't even seen the son of a bitch yet an' he's already killed Josh an' Wilson, an' put Clyde in jail. It's like he's a goddamn ghost. . . ."

"No such thing as ghosts. He's just a man who'll bleed an' die if I get him in my gun sights."

"Maybe. Let's stick together an' go fetch our horses. I got this powerful itch to get the hell away from here."

"He could still be out back someplace, waitin' for us to show ourselves. He'll gun us down just like he did Wilson."

"What the hell are we gonna do, Frank?"

A longer silence.

"I've got an idea. Get your ass over here, Carmen. We've got somethin' we want you to do. . . ."

Slocum guessed Clanton would send the woman after the horses to bring them around to the front, figuring Slocum wouldn't harm a Mexican girl. The plan might just benefit him, if things went right.

He slipped away from the shed.

Silver light from the moon and stars showed enough detail of the cantina entrance, and of the pair of horses the woman led around from the rear. Slocum had a perfect vantage point. However, he had to wait until the outlaws mounted before he made his play, in order to make sure the girl did not get in the line of fire. He waited, his .44/.40 trained on the Agave, hiding behind a small burro cart sitting in front of an adobe hut roughly a hundred yards from the front of the cantina.

As Slocum figured two men came out carrying rifles, each one covering a different direction with the muzzle of his gun as they approached the horses. They took the reins on a bay and a black, using the horses as shields.

The Mexican girl ran inside, and now things were set the way Slocum wanted them. It was unlikely he could avoid any shooting, judging that Frank Clanton was the type who wouldn't give up without a fight.

One outlaw mounted slowly, twisting his head back and

forth with his rifle sweeping the roadway. The second man swung aboard and reined his horse south, headed in the direction of the burro cart.

Perfect, Slocum thought.

Both men urged their horses forward at a walk, guns at the ready. When they were in good pistol range, Slocum rose above one wheel of the cart and aimed at the riders.

"Hold it there, boys! I can kill both of you real easy!" he cried.

The heavier of the two horsemen jerked his rifle at Slocum and fired. The boom of his gun thundered up and down the street, the bullet singing high above Slocum's head, and now he was sure he had no chance to end this peacefully.

He fired at the stocky outlaw, aiming for his shoulder, and heard the snap of gristle and bone above the bang of his Colt. The robber cried out, twisting in the saddle, dropping his rifle to the ground as he grabbed his shoulder. The bay horse underneath him spooked when it heard the second explosion, wheeling away from the noise. But Slocum's six-gun was already sighted in on the second rider, as the man he'd shot slid off his horse and collapsed on the caliche road, moaning, his legs thrashing in agony.

"Don't try it!" Slocum bellowed to the man atop the black. "I swear I'll kill you if you do!"

The outlaw drew back on his reins, and Slocum knew the man was weighing his chances, still clamping his Winchester to his shoulder while he stared at the burro cart, trying to find a target in the half-dark.

"Shit!" he heard the robber say under his breath. Then the man let his rifle fall and held up his hands. "Okay, stranger. I give up. Don't shoot."

Slocum came slowly around to the front of the cart expecting a trick, a sudden move by the outlaw to grab his pistol. "Just so you understand me, "Slocum said." I can't miss being this close. You ain't got anybody backing you now . . . it's just you and me, and I'm the one holding a gun. Only a damn fool would try it."

When the robber made no attempt to go for his gun, Slocum walked over to him, the muzzle of his Colt aimed, steady. "Get down," he commanded. "Do it slow, or you're gonna develop a leak just like your pardner laying there beside you."

Slocum watched the rider get down from his saddle, letting his horse wander off while he held his hands in the air. He had a square-jawed face and hard black eyes.

"Who the hell are you?" the outlaw asked when Slocum bent forward to pull the gun out of his holster.

"I'm John Slocum, not that it matters. I figure you're Frank Clanton, and you're wanted over in Texas for robbing the Texas and Pacific."

The outlaw blinked as Slocum backed away a half step with his pistol. "Never heard of you," Clanton said. "How in the hell did you find us?"

"I'll tell you all about it on our way over to the Eagle Pass jail. Turn around and keep them hands high. I'm gonna toss your pardner over his saddle, but my gun's on you the whole time. If you twitch, or rub your goddamn nose, I'll kill you. You're worth just as much to me dead as you are alive. Keep that in mind, Clanton. A dead man's easier to handle anyway . . ."

Three *federales* rounded a corner between the Agave cantina and the Rio Grande, blocking Slocum's path. The soldiers saw what was happening, and held a conference Slocum couln't hear from such a distance.

Clanton noticed the *federales*. "You ain't gonna get us back across that river," he said. "Cap'n Vela, the *federale* in charge here, is a friend of mine."

"And Comandante Porfirio Valdez in Villa Acuna is a friend of mine, so I figure I'll get you across all right. Comandante Valdez outranks Capitan Vela, and when I contact the *comandante* I'll let go. Same might not be said for you, Clanton. You got two things going against you."

"How's that?"

"You got an itchy trigger finger after you found your dead pardner and went and shot one of the *capitan*'s men. He ain't gonna be happy to hear it."

"You seen it happen?"

"Sure did. I was across the road. When I tell Comandante Valdez about it, whoever done the killing will face charges in the Mexican State of Coahuila for killing a soldier. That means you."

"What's . . . that other thing?"

"A helluva big reward being offered by the Texas and Pacific Railroad for you, and when I mention that thousand-dollar reward to Capitan Vela, I figure he'll contact the railroad and claim it for himself."

But just as Slocum finished what he was saying, he saw the three soldiers turn and hurry off down a side street. A slow smile crossed Slocum's face. "Looks like they've decided to let me take you and your wounded pardner back, Clanton. It don't appear they aim to do anything to stop me."

"Shit," Clanton said again, his shoulders dropping just a bit.

"That pretty well describes the condition you're in right now, Clanton. Up to your neck in it."

The wounded outlaw groaned again and sat up unsteadily, gripping his bleeding shoulder. "Jesus this hurts, Frank," he said when he looked over. "I gotta get to a sawbones or I'm liable to bleed to death."

"Shut up, Sonny. When this fella hauls us across that river we're both gonna hang."

"Hang?" Sonny said it between clenched teeth, fighting the pain from his wound.

Slocum added his reassurances. "Ain't much doubt about it, gentlemen. You killed United States soldiers and men who worked for the railroad in every robbery, not to mention the innocent passengers who died. I don't see any way either one of you can escape a date with the hangman." He grinned savagely. "But you still have a choice.

You can try to escape, if you feel lucky. You might just be able to outrun a bullet.''

Sonny's eyes turned to Clanton. "He's got us, Frank. Just do like he says an' don't try nothin'. I gotta get some morphine for my damn shoulder, 'cause this hurts like hell an' I'm bleeding worse'n all get-out.''

Clanton looked over his shoulder, his gaze falling to Slocum's gun. "Looks like we're dead either way.''

A thought occurred to Slocum as he stepped carefully over to the outlaw named Sonny, to help him to his feet and take his gun out of his holster. "I can ask the railroad to tell the judge to give you leniency . . . if you tell me who's giving Rose Miller the dates when those trains run.''

Clanton seemed edgy. "Let's do our talkin' when we make it over that river yonder. Vela's liable to put us in front of a damn firin' squad.''

"Just one more thing before we go,'' Slocum said, reaching into a pocket of Sonny's bloodstained denims where a bulge of currency was easy to see. "I want all the money first. I've got Sonny's share, Clanton, and now I want yours.''

"I keep it in my boot.''

"Then sit your ass down and pull the boot off. Hand over every last cent, because I'm gonna search both of you real good when we get to Eagle Pass.''

Clanton sat down grudgingly to pull off his left stovepipe boot. A sack of gold coins and a bundle of bank notes fell out on the ground.

"Now get up slow,'' Slocum said. "Help Sonny up on his horse, and then you climb up behind him to hold him in the saddle. I'll ride your black back across, and so help me if either one of you tries anything, I'm filling both of you full of holes. I'll be right behind you.''

Clanton went over to Sonny's horse and caught its reins. Then he grabbed Sonny by the seat of his pants to push him up on the bay's back. Slocum mounted the black as Clanton pulled up behind the cantle of Sonny's saddle.

"Now ride for that river," Slocum ordered. "And when we hit the other side, I want a name, the name of the man who's giving Rose Miller the information about those trains. If I don't hear a name by the time we get to the Texas side, I'm gonna start shooting till this pistol is empty. I'll tell Sheriff Wheeler you were both trying to escape."

Sonny, using his good arm, turned his horse toward the Rio Grande. Slocum fell in behind them.

No soldiers were waiting for them at the crossing. Slocum knew Paco would bring his thoroughbred over to Eagle Pass as soon as the boy learned what had taken place.

22

A blacksmith from the Eagle Pass Livery treated Sonny Jones's wound, for the town was too small to have a doctor and the smithy knew a thing or two about injured horses. Sheriff Ben Wheeler looked on until the blacksmith bandaged the bullet hole.

"Went clean through, so he'll probably be okay, Sheriff," the blacksmith said as Slocum ushered Sonny back to the single jail cell.

"Appreciate it, Doyle," the sheriff said, locking the cell door while the smithy walked out of the office carrying bottles of liniment and rags.

Paco stood in a corner of the office, beaming when he looked down at the silver coins in his palm. The boy had brought the stud across two hours before sunrise.

"That about does it then," Slocum said. He glared through the bars at Frank Clanton a moment.

"You said you got most of the railroad's money back," the sheriff remarked.

"Damn near all of it. They only had time to spend a few hundred dollars before I caught up to 'em."

"It's a wonder," Wheeler said, looking Slocum up and down, "how one man coulda got all six of 'em."

Slocum didn't bother correcting the lawman as to the

right count. "I need to send a wire to the Fort Worth office to let 'em know how things turned out. I reckon they'll be glad to hear the news."

Wheeler nodded. "Mostly, once a lawbreaker gits across that stretch of water, he's free as a bird. Even most of the bounty hunters won't go over there an' tangle with nobody, 'cause Cap'n Vela makes it rough on 'em."

"Vela's soldiers had a little morale problem last night. Didn't seem they wanted part of the fight. One of your guests here in this jail shot a *federale* by mistake. Seems Mr. Clanton got nervous and pulled his trigger too soon, thinking it was me he was shooting."

"It's a wonder Vela didn't order his men to kill Clanton after that."

"Like I said, the *federales* I saw were sure trying to find a way to avoid getting shot at."

Slocum turned for the office door. "You said the wire came about an hour ago, saying the Rangers were coming down to pick up your prisoners?"

"That's right. A Captain Ford signed the telegram, sayin' they'd be here sometime tomorrow to put irons on 'em an' take 'em back to San Antone."

Slocum saw Clanton watching him, gripping the bars with both hands, a steely look in his eyes. "Don't open that cell door for any reason, Sheriff. I'd stay until the Rangers got here, but I got some important information about how the robberies took place, and I need to get to San Antone as quick as that bay stud will carry me, to tie up a few loose ends."

"Loose ends?"

"Seems a couple more folks were involved in robbing those trains. I was pretty sure who one of 'em was, and now I know the other name I need."

"I ain't openin' this jail door till the Rangers show up," Wheeler reassured him. "You can count on it."

Slocum shook hands with the sheriff, and as he made to

go outside he tossled Paco's hair. "Thanks for all your help, my friend," he said.

"*Muchas gracias* for the money, Señor. I will tell Isabela what you say, that you see her again sometime when you come back to Piedras Negras."

"I'll be obliged," he said, walking out under a brilliant mid-morning sun, heading across the street to the telegraph office.

He prepared a telegram to Malcom Warren in care of the Texas and Pacific Railroad Company in Fort Worth:

OLD FRIEND **STOP** GOT FIVE THOUSAND FOUR HUN-
DRED DOLLARS BACK FROM CLANTON **STOP** CLANTON
AND TWO MORE IN JAIL **STOP** OTHERS DEAD I KNOW
WHERE INFORMATION CAME FROM **STOP** WILL WIRE
FROM SAN ANTONIO AS SOON AS SHERIFF DAWSON AR-
RESTS PARTIES INVOLVED **STOP** SLOCUM **END**

He paid for the wire and went out to his horse, preparing for a long, dusty ride north to San Antone. With both can- teens full to cross more desert country, a fresh bottle of whiskey, and a handful of cigars to go along with the jerky and tortillas he'd bought at a general store, he was as ready for the trip as he'd ever be.

Once, riding out of town, he looked over his shoulder as he thought about pretty Isabela. Maybe he would come back after all, just to get to know her better.

Gazing north at a brush-choked desert, he knew he'd left a hundred towns behind him like this, most with a pretty woman on his mind. It was his nature, the way John Slocum was made.

He rubbed the stud's neck and asked it for a long trot, for soon the heat of the day would descend upon this barren wasteland and he wouldn't punish his horse any more than necessary.

He had a surprise coming for two people in the city of San Antonio, one a beautiful woman and the other a man who was in cahoots with her—and Frank Clanton. Slocum wanted to see the look of surprise on Rose Miller's face when he told her what he knew, and what had happened to Frank and her share of the money they were taking, with the help of an accomplice. But he needed to know one more thing before asking Sheriff Dawson to make the arrests. Was the man who had been telling her about the payroll schedules doing so without realizing what he'd done, or was he getting a cut of the profits?

Slocum wouldn't know until he got to San Antonio and talked to Rose, and while he was at it he considered the wisdom of bedding her one more time, before she went to prison. While it might be considered an ungentlemanly thing to do, it was what she deserved for being involved in a scheme to rob the army and the railroad. And taking her to bed one more time was hardly an unpleasant notion.

Miles of empty range lay before him. He settled back in the saddle for a long ride, which gave him plenty of time to make up his mind about bedding Rose one more time.

23

Slocum knocked softly on Rose Miller's upstairs bedroom door. Sheriff Ike Dawson stood behind him in the poorly lit hallway above the Velvet Slipper. The sheriff hadn't been too willing to believe him right at first when he'd informed him of what Frank Clanton had said about Rose's involvement in the robberies.

"It's gonna be hard to convince a judge she was in on it," he had said.

"I heard Clanton's confession. I'll testify to it in court if I have to."

"I imagine Judge Carson will let you sign a statement to that effect. But somebody has to be tellin' her when the trains with the payroll will run through Devil's River Canyon. It has to be somebody with the railroad company, seems like, or someone who knows what day the army is sendin' it and exactly what train it's gonna be on."

"That's what we aim to find out tonight," Slocum had said. "We'll have to watch the Velvet Slipper and see who goes up to her room when I plant the information in two sets of hands, the two men I suspect. One of 'em will try to talk to her, to get her to keep her mouth shut, and that'll be our man, the one who told her about the payroll schedules. I'm expecting whoever it is to use the back door, so nobody'll see him. I'll keep a watch on the alleyway, if you'll put a deputy out front, and as soon as we see who her visitor is, I'll send your deputy for you to make the arrest.''

"You said you ran into Cap'n Ford an' his men on the way up from Eagle Pass?''

"They're bringing Clanton and two of his boys back to toss them in the county jail. That's another thing I'm aiming to tell my two suspects . . . that Clanton is on his way to jail, and he don't aim to go to prison by himself. He's naming names. He intends to take somebody with him, meaning Rose and the two members of his gang I stuck in the Eagle Pass jail. But there has to be one more, the informant, and I've got two strong suspects.''

"How come you got just two suspects?'' Dawson had asked, in a way that suggested he had a longer list.

"Something Clanton told me. I'll put it all in a deposition when I give my statement to the judge.''

"But how come Clanton don't know who Rose gets her information from?''

"Rose never told him. It was her insurance policy, to make sure she always got her share. Clanton needed her, in order to keep robbing the right trains. She only told him that her source was reliable.''

"Hell, that ain't enough to narrow it down to just two men, is it?''

"She let it slip one time when Frank came to see her to give over her share, months after the second robbery. The man who was giving her the information is married, so she told Clanton, and at times he's someone directly responsible for custody of the payroll. He sneaks off at night to bed down with Rose. I did a little bit of checking. Colonel Bush and Sergeant Baker are both single. That boils down to two men who know when the money's leaving, are responsible for the money's safety at various times, and who have wives.''

Thus it was that Slocum and Sheriff Dawson stood in

front of Rose's door tonight, after Slocum had seen one of
his prime suspects go through the back door of the Velvet
Slipper, a man who'd needed to tell Rose of Clanton's capture and that he was talking about others involved. Slocum
made sure he'd told both suspects earlier in the evening,
while paying a visit to their offices, that Clanton had been
captured and he was naming Rose Miller as his accomplice
in all the robberies. The guilty man would know he had to
stop Rose from naming him as the source of the payroll
information. But what Slocum was still unsure of was
whether or not the guilty party had told her what she
wanted to know as a part of the plan, or innocently, persuaded by her boundless womanly charms.

"Who is it?" a muffled woman's voice asked from beyond the bedroom door.

"John Slocum," he said, wondering if Rose's visitor
would try to jump out her window to avoid being seen,
even though it was a second-floor room. As a precaution,
Sheriff Dawson's chief deputy, Jory Turner, was standing
outside, keeping an eye on a narrow space between the
saloon and a single-story hatmaker's shop.

A rustling noise made Slocum tense, wondering if the
man with Rose had a gun. Slocum rested his palm on the
butt of his Colt to be ready, just in case.

A silence passed. Then Rose spoke to him without opening her door. "Sorry, John, but I'm . . . busy tonight. I have
a . . . gentleman caller. Please come back another evening.
Maybe tomorrow, when I don't have company."

"I have some company too, Rose. Sheriff Dawson is
with me. Open the door."

"Sheriff Dawson? Why is Ike there?"

"I'm afraid you already know why, Rose. Make things
easier and open the door. The sheriff also needs to ask your
gentleman caller a few questions. We know who he is."

Another, much longer silence. Slocum heard whispered
voices in the bedroom, yet he couldn't quite make out what
was being said or who was doing the whispering.

He decided to add a further warning. "Tell your friend not to bother with the window. Deputy Turner is down there with a shotgun."

Sheriff Dawson was growing impatient. "Open up, Rose, or we'll have to break it down!"

"I'm . . . I'm not decent yet, Sheriff. Please give me a moment to get dressed."

Slocum smiled inwardly, remembering Rose's beautiful naked body vividly.

"Hurry it up, Rose," Dawson added, scowling, moving his right hand to his holstered pistol, resting it there. "No sense in waitin'. You know I'm gonna have to arrest you because of what Frank Clanton told Mr. Slocum. Open the goddamn door or I swear I'm gonna bust it down! An' tell Mr. Herring not to try nothin' stupid, like pullin' a gun on us. We've gotta ask him a few questions."

Slocum wondered if the banker might be dumb enough to make a jump from the upper-floor window, despite the knowledge that a deputy was waiting down below. Slocum hadn't been able to read the man very well during their first meeting, although he did have a sense that Herring was indeed hiding something. But was it only that he was seeing Rose in secret? Or was he in on the scheme himself? Herring had protested his innocence when Slocum came to the bank, claiming he could have stolen the money any time he wanted by simply opening the bank vault. But that would point a finger at him, whereas the train robberies made Frank Clanton the wanted man. Herring, and Rose Miller, had the answers he needed to solve the riddle, how Clanton *knew* which trains to rob.

"Okay," Rose said, as the lock on her door rattled. She opened it just a crack and peered out, glancing at Slocum, then at Sheriff Dawson. "You can't prove anything on me," she added quickly. "It's Frank's word against mine. I won't admit to a thing. We're barely acquainted. . . ."

Slocum, his hand still on his gun, pushed the door inward gently. The oil lamp beside Rose's bed was turned down low, but even in dim light he could see the banker standing beside the open window. Herring's hands were empty, and Slocum relaxed a bit. It appeared Herring wasn't going to try to shoot his way out of the room, or jump, risking serious injury if he landed wrong, although he was standing very close to the windowsill, as if the thought of jumping had occurred to him when he'd learned who was outside in the hallway.

Rose was wearing a silky red nightgown, closed around her slender waist by a sash. Her hair was mussed and some of the red paint was smeared on her lips. Slocum gave her a polite nod and walked into the room, fixing his gaze on the banker.

Sheriff Dawson came in behind Slocum, speaking first to Rose. "Put a dress on, Rose. I've gotta take you down to county jail an' you can't go dressed like this."

"I didn't *do* anything!" she snapped. "I don't care what Frank told anybody. He's a liar!"

"You can explain it to the county attorney when they take you in front of Judge Carson. Now walk over yonder behind that dressin' screen an' put on somethin' decent."

Rose adopted a pouty expression, but the sheriff pointed to a dressing screen in a corner of her room, and she wheeled for it without a word.

Slocum addressed Herring. "Let's hear your side of it, Mr. Herring. Are you and Rose in with Frank Clanton on this together?"

"You have me in an embarrassing position, Mr. Slocum. I am a . . . married man, found in a single woman's bedroom." He was in shirtsleeves, his white shirt only partly buttoned, and his dress pants had suspenders he'd forgotten to pull over his shoulders.

"Right now, that's the least of your worries," Slocum told him.

"Precisely what do you mean?"

"I'm sure you know what I mean, but we'll play this out if it's the way you want it. Did you tell Rose about the army payroll shipments and when they were leaving on the Texas and Pacific because you're in on it?''

Herring glanced over at the dressing screen. "Every now and then she did ask about my . . . my responsibilities, like how I felt being in charge of so much money at the bank. It's more cash than we usually have, when the army is preparing to send its payroll out to far western outposts by rail. Perhaps a few times she did ask when the money was leaving." Herring swallowed hard. "When you came to my office the first time, I gathered that you suspected me of complicity in the robberies. I began to remember things I had said to her, and questions she'd asked. I came over to see her as soon as you left the bank, to question her myself, to see if she could possibly have been involved in the robberies by telling this Frank Clanton about it when I mentioned a shipment leaving by rail.''

His eyes flickered to the dressing curtain again, and then back to Slocum. "When I confronted her," he went on, "she told me she would blackmail me, that she'd tell my wife and the bank's board of directors about my visiting her, and accuse me of knowingly being a part of these holdups. I'd be ruined in San Antonio, and with the bank, and I could face prosecution if a judge and a jury believed her. She said Frank Clanton would back her story about me, that I was giving them every detail of the army shipments. I had no choice but to remain silent . . . until today, when you came to see me again. I came to beg her to tell the truth, that she'd threatened me with blackmail after I confronted her with my suspicions. She laughed in my face and threatened to expose me to my wife and the bank board, unless I kept my mouth shut." He sighed. "And then I allowed her to seduce me again tonight. I've been caught red-handed, it seems. However, I did not know until it was too late that she had been using me all along, pretending to care for me and understand my . . . rather difficult marriage.''

Sheriff Dawson nodded. "I'd never have figured it of you, Mr. Herring."

"I'm a weak man, I suppose, when it comes to matters of the flesh. Rose and I have been partners in this saloon for a number of years and so I trusted her, never once wondering why she asked me about the payroll shipments. I was utterly fooled by her."

Slocum heard the soft scrape of a foot behind them, and then the deadly metallic click of a gun being cocked. He was careful when he turned around slowly, for it was suddenly clear that Rose had tricked them, both him and Sheriff Dawson.

Rose was standing at one corner of the dressing screen with a .32-caliber revolver in her hands, dressed in denim riding pants, a man's shirt, and boots. She aimed the gun at Slocum, waving it back and forth between him and the sheriff. "Sorry, boys," she said coldly, her pale eyes suddenly transformed into slitted windows of hate. "I'm not going to jail. Let me warn you that I've used a gun several times and I'm a good shot, so don't try anything dumb. First you, Slocum, you take your pistol out with your thumb and forefinger and let it drop on the floor. Then it's your turn, Ike, and I promise I'll kill either one or both of you if you don't do exactly like I say."

Slocum grinned. "You'll get no trouble out of me, pretty lady. I'm not looking for a way to die young." He took his gun out just as she'd told him to, and let it land on the floorboards with a hollow thud.

"Damn, Rose," Sheriff Dawson complained, "you ain't gonna get away with this." But even as he said it, he carefully took out his pistol and let it fall to the floor.

"That's better," she said, her voice changed, harder than Slocum could have imagined coming from such a beautiful young woman. She took a key from her pocket. "I'm taking your guns and locking all three of you inside this room. You'll have to jump out that window, or break the door down, and that's all the time I'll need. Don't try to follow me, because I'll kill any of you who gets too close. I'm leaving town."

"You'll never make it, Rose," Sheriff Dawson said. "We'll have to follow you no matter where you try to hide."

"I'll take my chances," she snapped. "Now back away from those pistols."

Slocum and the sheriff followed her instructions. Rose bent down, covering them with her .32 the entire time, to scoop their guns off the floor.

She backed away to the door, sticking both extra pistols in the waistband of her pants. "Remember, I'll shoot anyone who tries to follow me," she said. Then she closed the door quickly and locked it.

Slocum heard her light footsteps running down the hall. He turned to Dawson. "I'll go get her," he said, reaching inside his shirt for his bellygun. "She won't get very far. . . ."

24

He had shattered the door frame and the simple lock with
his shoulder on the first try, racing down the hallway, then
the stairs two at a time. A few patrons of the Velvet Slipper
were still looking at the bat-wing doors swinging back and
forth when he reached the bottom of the stairs, pistol in
hand.

Slocum ran outside, just in time to catch a glimpse of
Rose turning west down a dark side street, her feet flying.

"This is gonna be too easy," he muttered, breaking into
a hard run after her.

He saw her again when he rounded the corner, blond
hair a guidepost to her escape route even in the darkness.
Slocum ran faster, closing the distance, keeping to the
darkest spots along the empty roadway.

Just as quickly he knew where she was headed . . . the
livery stable where he kept his horse not far from the St.
Anthony Hotel. She wouldn't have time to saddle an animal
before he got there, and by slipping around to the back he'd
have a chance to jump her while she was occupied with the
saddling.

Once, Rose looked over her shoulder as she ran, but it
was a fleeting glance, her mind set on running as fast as

she could, and he was certain she hadn't seen him in the shadows.

She was pulling the cinch strap tight when he crept up on her from an empty stall with its gate hanging open. She had all three pistols stuck in her pants, needing both hands to get a big blue roan gelding saddled.

He grabbed her from behind in a bear hug, clamping her arms to her sides.

"You bastard!" she screamed, kicking, trying to pound his arms with her tiny fists.

"Hold still, darlin'," he whispered in her ear, reaching for the guns she carried, tossing them down on the straw covering the stable floor one at a time, holstering his own prize Colt .44/.40 while holding her with one arm.

After he'd disarmed her, he swung her around, grinning in the light from a kerosene lantern hanging in the saddle shed. "You ain't going anyplace, Rose, so stop fighting me." He seized her wrists in an iron grip.

She tried to kick him in the leg, although he dodged it easily.

"Let me go!" she cried, anger hardening her features. "I can make it worth your while. . . ." she added in a much softer voice.

He shook his head, refusing her offer. "No, thanks, ma'am. I've had all I want from you, and more besides. You're good in bed, and I'm sure that's what trapped poor old Herring into saying things he hadn't oughta. But I'm not letting you go, not for all the money you've got, or all the pleasure hidden between those pretty legs."

"You arrogant son of a bitch! What makes you think I'd ever sleep with you again?"

"You would, if I offered to get you out of town."

She stopped resisting a moment. "I'd do it, John," she said in a far gentler manner. "I promise to give you all of me you'd ever want for the rest of your life if you'll just help me get away from here."

"No, thanks, darlin'. I've already had all of you I want, like I told you before."

"Please!" she whimpered, staring up into his face.

"Sorry. You broke the law, and you almost cost a good friend of mine a lot of business for his railroad. No deals."

"I'll be in prison for years," she begged. "Frank made me do it, I swear."

"Tell it to the judge, Rose. Maybe he'll listen better than I am."

He was grateful there had been no need for a gun or a bullet when he'd corralled her. It would have been a shame to put any holes in such beautiful skin, even if the soft skin was covering a black heart.

He picked up his .44/.40 and led her by the arm out of the livery, turning toward Sheriff Dawson's office and the Bexar County jail. Rose came quietly, her head bowed, and he noticed a trace of a tear on her cheeks as he took her toward the center of town.

"Please let me go," she said one final time.

"I think you know what my answer is, Rose. Too bad that a beautiful lady like you had to cross over the line. Seems like a helluva waste . . ."

Malcom Warren, fresh off the train from Fort Worth, ordered Slocum and himself another round of brandy at the St. Anthony Hotel dining room. Claire was waiting on their table, and every time when she came over she gave Slocum a secret smile.

"So tell me, John," Malcom continued, "how were you able to narrow it down to Sheldon Herring and Willard Clifton? That's the part you left out."

"Something Clanton told me, something he heard from Rose one time, that her information came from a married man who slipped out now and then to see her. I checked my other suspects at Fort Sam Houston and found out they were single. Herring and Clifton were the only ones with wives."

"I suspected it was Willard all along," Malcom said, taking a sip of the fresh glasses of brandy Claire brought them. "But in my heart of hearts I still wondered. Willard has been with us for years. An exemplary record with the company. Then all of a sudden, these robberies start happening out of this San Antonio office. I had to consider him a suspect. However, I'll admit I never thought the bank was involved."

"It wasn't really. Herring was so taken with Rose Miller he let his guard down. She's a beautiful woman and Herring has a rotten marriage. So he visited her, and told her things without realizing how she was using him, or that Rose had ties to a man who robbed banks and trains for a living."

"You did a marvelous job, John, wrapping this whole thing up so quickly and getting almost all of our money back. I'm paying you the one-thousand-dollar reward, as well as your expenses coming down."

"Keep the reward, Malcom. We're friends. I may need a big favor from you one of these days. Just cover my expenses and we'll call it square."

"Nonsense. You earned every penny of it."

"I won't take it. Just make the arrangements so I can ship my horse back to Denver with me by rail. I'm worn down and so is my stud. The train ride will give us both a chance to rest up a bit."

"Consider it done. When will you be leaving?"

"Tomorrow, if you can book passage for me and my horse. I have a little business to take care of tonight."

"More business? I thought you said. . . ." He saw Slocum look at Claire. "Ah, now I understand, John. You haven't changed a bit."

"Don't intend to, not till I'm too old to live my life the way I've been living it."

"You're the damnedest womanizer I ever knew, John Slocum. I never saw a man who was any better at it."

"Takes practice," he replied, giving Claire a wink as

she went past their table carrying a tray of food to other customers in the dining room.

Malcom chuckled. "From what I've heard about you, you've had plenty of that," he said, puffing on his cigar. "It would appear you have more practice planned for this evening."

"That I do," Slocum said, looking forward to another swim in the river with Claire . . . if what he aimed to do with her could be called swimming.

J. R. ROBERTS
THE GUNSMITH